D0058363

The Silver Door

The Silver Door

EMILY RODDA

 Scholastic Press • *New York*

Library of Congress Cataloging-in-Publication Data

Rodda, Emily.
The silver door / Emily Rodda. — 1st [American] ed.
p. cm. — (The Three doors trilogy; bk 2)
Originally published: Parkside, S. Aust.: Omnibus Books, 2012.
Summary: Rye has defeated the sorcerer Olt, freed the island of Dorne, and rescued one of his brothers, but when he returns to the city of Weld with his three companions, he finds that very little has changed — the skimmer monsters still attack at night and the Warden is behaving very strangely.
ISBN 978-0-545-42992-4
1. Magic — Juvenile fiction. 2. Quests (Expeditions) — Juvenile fiction. 3. Monsters — Juvenile fiction. 4. Brothers — Juvenile fiction. 5. Adventure stories. [1. Magic — Fiction. 2. Monsters — Fiction. 3. Brothers — Fiction. 4. Adventure and adventurers — Fiction.] I. Title.
PZ7.R5996Sil 2013
823.914 — dc23
2012017545

10 9 8 7 6 5 4 3 2 1   13 14 15 16 17

Printed in the U.S.A.   23

First American edition, April 2013

The text was set in Palatino.

CONTENTS

MIDSUMMER DAY

The sorcerer Olt was dead. The island of Dorne was free of his tyranny at last. As the sun rose on Midsummer Day, Oltan city seethed with rejoicing people. Olt's red banners lay trampled in the narrow streets. The dread stone fortress that for so long had glared over Oltan bay and out to the Sea of Serpents was a smoking ruin.

Olt had boasted that he would live forever, but Midsummer Eve had proved him wrong. Now, wild with relief and joy, most people were giving little thought to his other great boast — that his power threw a charmed circle around Dorne, protecting it from invasion by the Lord of Shadows in the west.

And Rye, the boy who had ended the tyrant's reign of terror, was not thinking of Olt at all. Invisible beneath a magic hood that concealed him and everyone he touched, Rye was slipping quietly out of the smoke-filled

1

city. The three he had saved from a terrible death — his friend Sonia, his brother Dirk, and Dirk's sweetheart, Faene of Fleet — were by his side. His mind was fixed on home.

As the sun climbed higher and the hours passed, some drinkers in the packed taverns of Oltan began to wonder why Olt's conqueror had not yet appeared among them, to claim their thanks. Others thought they knew and, over brimming tankards, loudly shared their views with anyone who would listen.

The hero of Midsummer Eve, these wise ones said, was on his way back to the east coast of Dorne, to report the success of his mission. The east was wild and barren, but there, it was rumored, Olt's exiled younger brother had established a stronghold seven years before. If a boy with blazing red hair and magic at his command had not come from the exiles' camp, where had he come from?

So the wise ones said — with perfect confidence, too. They would have been astounded to learn that Rye and his companions were in fact moving swiftly toward Dorne's center, sped by a charmed ring, their goal an ancient walled city deep within the forbidden Fell Zone. The people of Oltan had never heard of Weld. They did not dream that any such place existed. As far as they knew, the dark forest at Dorne's heart sheltered only monstrous beasts and the strange, magic beings called Fellan, who were best left well alone.

Only the four who had fled the city at first light could have told them differently, and it was far too late for that. By late morning, Rye, Sonia, Dirk, and Faene were already halfway to the Fell Zone and entering the deserted town of Fleet.

Rye, Dirk, and Sonia were anxious to reach the Fell Zone well before nightfall, but they had broken their journey for Faene's sake. Faene knew that her people had fled Dorne. She knew that her town had been abandoned. Still, she could not pass it without a glance. She wanted to visit her parents' grave. She wanted to say good-bye.

Fleet was a sad place now. A message of farewell had been scrawled on the sign that had once welcomed visitors. The horse fields were deserted. The graceful houses with their tall chimneys were closed and shuttered. The Fleet clinks, the little creatures whose ancestors had long ago hollowed out mighty rocks to make those chimneys, chattered in empty fireplaces, wondering where the people, and the people's tasty food scraps, had gone.

The courtyard garden in the Fleet guesthouse looked as peaceful as when Rye had first seen it. The bell tree in the center stretched its branches over Faene as she knelt by the long, flat stone that marked her parents' resting place.

As Rye gazed at the tree, pictures of home crowded his mind. His mother tending her beehives.

His brother Dirk, home from work on the Wall, shouting a greeting as he swung through the garden gate. His other brother Sholto in the house, bent over his books after a long day helping Tallus the healer. Himself, the youngest, yawning over schoolwork in the shade of the bell tree that all his life had marked the passing of the seasons with its blossoms, new leaves, golden fruit, bare brown branches . . .

That tree was gone — destroyed by the ravenous winged beasts called skimmers that flew over the Wall of Weld every night in summer, to hunt warm flesh.

Rye touched the sturdy stick he carried in his belt. It was all that remained of his family's bell tree — all that remained of his old life.

His eyes stung. Looking hastily away from the tree, he caught a glimpse of the kneeling Faene and blinked back his tears. What was he thinking of, giving way to self-pity when Faene had lost so much?

There was no point in mourning his old, safe Weld life. Like the family bell tree, that life was gone — and gone for good, unless the skimmer attacks could be stopped.

For seven long summers, Weld had been a place of fear. Thousands of people and animals had died. Homes and crops had been destroyed. And the Warden of Weld had been exposed as the timid, stubborn leader he was. Only after there had been riots had he acted, challenging Weld's heroes to go beyond the Wall and seek the Enemy who was sending the skimmers.

Hundreds of brave volunteers had answered the Warden's call and left the city. None had returned. All had been declared dead — including Dirk and Sholto.

But I found Dirk, Rye thought, glancing at his brother, whose eyes were fixed on Faene. *Now Dirk, Sonia, and I will find Sholto. And this time we will find the source of the skimmers as well.*

He pushed away the doubts that had begun to shadow his mind whenever he thought of Sholto. Since leaving Weld, he had not dreamed of Sholto once. And it had been his vivid dreams of both his brothers that had convinced him they were alive, somewhere outside the Wall.

Sholto still lives, Rye told himself fiercely. *Sholto is clever and as agile as Dirk is strong. It means nothing that I have not dreamed of him lately. My mind has been full of other things. So much has happened. . . .*

He raised his hand to the little brown bag hanging by its faded cord around his neck.

We were given this in trust for you, the Fellan Edelle had said when she showed him the bag. *It contains nine powers to aid you in your quest.*

Rye knew the Fellan had mistaken him for someone else, but by now, he felt no more than a tiny twinge of guilt for accepting the powers. Without them, he would never have been able to save Dirk, Sonia, and Faene. Fingering the bag, feeling the familiar tingling of the magic inside it, he thought about the powers he had discovered so far.

The crystal that gave light and also allowed him to see through solid objects. The horsehair ring for speed. The hood that made him invisible. The sea serpent scale that allowed him to swim in the roughest water . . .

Great powers, all of them — and only Rye could use them, though he could share them with anyone who touched him.

But what of the other charms in the bag — the red feather, the snail shell, the tiny golden key, the paper-wrapped sweet that smelled of honey? Rye still did not know what they could do. He had an idea about one of them, however, and if he was right . . .

"I wish you would tell me how you came by that sorcerer's bag, Rye," Dirk said quietly.

Rye jumped as his brother's voice broke into his thoughts. Dirk had turned to look at him and was eyeing the brown bag uneasily.

"Why will you not tell me?" Dirk persisted. "Did you steal it?"

"Of course not!" Rye protested, feeling the heat rise into his face. "But I swore I would not tell how I came by it, and I cannot break my promise. It is like your being unable to tell Faene about Weld, Dirk, because of the volunteers' oath of secrecy."

Dirk frowned. It infuriated him that because of his oath to the Warden it had been left to Sonia to tell Faene about Weld, about the skimmers, about the three magic Doors — gold, silver, and wood — that were the only way through the Wall.

"I swore no oath," Sonia had said. "And even if I had, it would not have stopped me telling you, Faene. After all, we are *taking* you to Weld! It is absurd not to *talk* about it. But Dirk and Rye are very law-abiding. People in Weld are, you will find. They like to follow rules. It is very tedious."

Faene had smiled uncertainly. Her soft blue eyes were wide — and no wonder! Like the people of Oltan, Faene had thought that Dirk, Rye, and Sonia came from the exiles' secret camp in the east. She had been prepared to follow Dirk there. Now she found that his home was an old, forgotten city that could only be reached by traveling through the forbidden forest she had feared all her life.

"But — why do you have to go back into Weld at all?" she had asked. "Why not just begin your search for Sholto and the skimmers from here?"

Dirk sighed. "I considered that. But I wished to see you settled safely in the Keep of Weld before I left you again, Faene. And Rye has persuaded me —"

"The Doors are *magic*, Faene," Rye broke in as the young woman turned her reproachful blue gaze on him. "They could lead . . . anywhere. The golden Door led Dirk here. But I am certain that Sholto would have chosen the silver Door. So to be sure of picking up his trail, we must go through the silver Door ourselves. Do you see?"

Faene looked doubtful. She glanced at Sonia, who cheerfully proceeded to make things worse.

"Of course, we will have to keep our return

secret," Sonia said. "I cannot imagine what the Warden would do if he heard we had brought a stranger through the Wall! He thinks you are all barbarians out here — and everyone else in Weld thinks so, too."

She shrugged at Faene's startled expression. "Of course, we know better now," she went on. "But the Warden will not listen to us. And, more important, he would certainly forbid Rye and Dirk to leave Weld again. He is obsessed with safety and would not allow them to risk their lives a second time. So we will climb up the chimney from the Chamber of the Doors, and I will lead you to a safe hiding place."

"Chimney?" Faene repeated blankly. Dirk scowled at Sonia, who grinned, but wisely said no more.

Faene had been very quiet ever since that conversation, and Dirk, Rye knew, feared that she was changing her mind about going to Weld. Rye suspected, too, that the nearer to the Fell Zone they came, the more Dirk wondered if he should be asking Faene to face its terrors. Dirk's only weapon, the great skimmer hook he had brought from Weld, had been taken from him after his capture in Olt's fortress. He had learned to trust Rye's speed ring and concealing hood. But would they be enough to keep Faene safe?

Looking at his brother's worried face now, Rye was tempted to tell him that the Fell Zone might not be the problem they feared. But as he hesitated, Faene stood up from the grave, Dirk went to meet her, and the moment passed.

It was just as well, Rye thought, following them from the courtyard with Sonia. He had not tested his idea. For all he knew, it was quite wrong. It might have been cruel to raise Dirk's hopes.

As they left the guesthouse, Faene glanced around as if she was searching for something. But there was nothing out of place. Everything was clean and bare. Outside, the stream that ran by the road babbled and sang on its way to the coast. The sound seemed very loud in the silence.

Faene turned to Dirk, her eyes swimming with tears. "I thought they might have left a message for me," she murmured. "Just in case I returned . . ."

Dirk put his arm around her. "They thought you were dead, Faene."

She nodded and pressed her cheek to his shoulder.

Rye turned quickly away and pretended to be interested in the scrawl on the welcome board.

WELCOME TO

FLEET

Home Of Dorne's Finest Horses

FArEwell dorNE! we have GOne TO FInd The priZe of FrEEdom.

Rye grimaced. The words barely made sense. The untidy writing, with its jumble of large and small letters, looked like the work of an overexcited child.

It was strange. Everything else in the deserted town had been left in perfect order. This sign was the only jarring note.

Something occurred to him. He looked at the words again, more closely. Then he laughed aloud.

Faene's head jerked up. She stared at Rye in hurt confusion. "I am sorry," she said rather stiffly, wiping her eyes. "I am being foolish, I know. But —"

"No, Faene!" Rye cried, stabbing his finger at the board. "Look! Nanion and the others did not forget you. They *did* leave you a message! But they disguised it! They must have felt they had to, for safety. They did not know Olt would die! Read the capital letters — just those!"

Faene blinked at the board.

"F-A-E-N-E . . ." Her jaw dropped.

Dirk whooped. Sonia exclaimed and clapped her hands.

Faene's face was a picture of wondering joy.

"FAENE!" she read. "GO TO FITZFEE."

THE FIFTH POWER

After that, Faene was as keen as everyone else to hurry on. But it was not because she wanted to reach the Fell Zone. It was because the FitzFee goat farm lay in the same direction.

"Why did I not think of FitzFee before?" she called to Dirk as they sped through the range of low hills beyond Fleet. "He was Nanion's good friend. And he was the one who brought you to us, Dirk, barely alive after the bloodhog attack. If it had not been for him, we would never have met!"

She seemed to have no doubt that they would go to the farm — even stay there for a day or two. And plainly Dirk thought there would be no harm in the delay, if it pleased Faene.

Rye felt very differently. Sorry as he was for Faene and happy as he would be to see Magnus FitzFee again, a feeling of urgency was growing within him.

With every step, the feeling became stronger. He had the sense that time was running out, and that every moment's delay was dangerous.

Dangerous for Sholto. Dangerous for Weld itself.

Rye was sure that Sonia felt the same way. She kept shooting frowning looks in his direction as if she was willing him to speak. But how could he ask Faene to ignore the message that had meant so much to her?

So he just ran on, past green fields and tiny villages, trying not to think, refusing to meet Sonia's eyes.

By the time the giant trees of the Fell Zone were looming ahead, however, his feeling of urgency had become almost unbearable. And as the companions turned to the left, where the Oltan road met the rutted track that ran beside the forest fringe, Sonia took matters into her own hands.

"The bridge that crosses the stream is ahead," she shouted over the sound of the wind. "That is where we left the Fell Zone. So that is where we should enter it, to return to Weld. Do you agree, Dirk?"

"Oh yes," Dirk answered stiffly, tightening his grip on Faene's hand. "When the time comes."

Sonia drew breath to reply. Rye slowed, pushed back the hood, and braced himself for an argument. And at that moment, a green cart drawn by an old brown horse rattled across the bridge and began trundling toward them.

"FitzFee!" Faene cried.

A stocky, child-sized figure stood up, waved wildly, and pulled on the horse's reins.

In moments, the four companions were gathered around FitzFee, who had jumped from the cart and was laughing and hugging each of them in turn.

"Bless my heart, how good it is to see you!" the small man bellowed. "I can't believe it! You saw the message, then, Faene? 'Just in case,' Nanion said to me. 'In case by some miracle she is safe.' And by all that's wonderful, here you are! Now! What's the meaning of all that smoke beyond the hills?"

So they told him. And it was pure joy to see light spread over his face as he realized Olt was gone for good.

"Alda always said it would happen one day!" he chortled. "Well — you hurry on to the farm and tell her how right she was. Ah, if only I could come with you! But I've got these dratted deliveries to make."

He waved his hand at his load, which was covered with wet sacking to keep it cool. "It's a pity, but butter, milk, and cheese won't keep in this heat, and that's all there is to it. I'll join you as soon as I can, and then we'll have a real celebration."

"FitzFee, I am not sure —" Rye began.

"Wait till you see what Nanion left in our care for you, Faene!" FitzFee chattered on, climbing nimbly back into the cart. "*Four* fine Fleet horses!"

Faene gasped and clasped her hands.

"Yes!" FitzFee beamed. "And you have a home

with us, dear girl, for as long as you like — though I daresay you'll be wanting a place of your own soon enough." He chuckled and looked meaningfully at Dirk.

Faene hesitated, warm color rising in her cheeks. "Dirk has to go away again, very soon," she murmured. "He and Rye — and Sonia, too — have something they have to do."

"Oh, I daresay, I daresay," said FitzFee, winking and tapping the side of his nose. "They want to carry the great news to El — ah, pardon — to the east, let's say, themselves. Well, you have horses to lend now, Faene, my dear! That will make their journey much faster. Safer, too."

His face grew serious. "And no more shortcuts through places no one in their senses would go, eh?" he muttered to Rye and Sonia, crossing his fingers and his wrists and jerking his head toward the Fell Zone.

Pretending not to notice the awkward silence that followed his warning, he picked up the horse's reins again.

"We'll be off, then," he said. "See you back at the farm!"

He clicked his tongue to the old mare, and the wagon rattled away, leaving the four travelers alone.

Rye and Sonia looked at each other. Dirk looked at Faene. Her head was bowed. She seemed to be lost in her own thoughts.

"Perhaps this makes a difference, Faene," Dirk murmured. "You would have a safe home with FitzFee. And there are the horses. Perhaps you would rather stay. . . ."

"And if I did, Dirk, would you come back for me?" Faene asked, without raising her head.

"I would try," Dirk said in a level voice. "But there is a chance I may be . . . prevented."

Indeed, Rye thought grimly. *If the Warden has anything to say about it, you will.*

Faene dipped into a pocket of her skirt and drew out a pencil and a water-stained notebook. She wrote for a moment, then tore out the page and handed it to Dirk.

Rye could see the note from where he stood. He read it, and a lump rose in his throat.

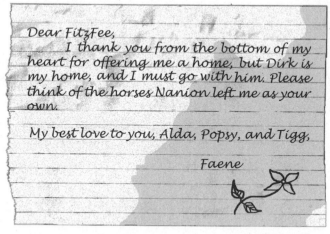

Dear FitzFee,
        I thank you from the bottom of my heart for offering me a home, but Dirk is my home, and I must go with him. Please think of the horses Nanion left me as your own.

My best love to you, Alda, Popsy, and Tigg,

Faene

"Are you sure, Faene?" Dirk said huskily.

"I am sure." Faene smiled at him, though tears were standing in her eyes. "I cannot risk losing you a second time, Dirk. And it is best this way — best not to go to the farm, I mean. They would ask too many questions we cannot answer."

She and Dirk went to place the note, weighed down by a stone, in the middle of the bridge where FitzFee would be sure to see it on his return journey.

While their backs were turned, Rye felt in the bag of powers and drew out the little red feather. There would never be a better time to test his idea.

Up! he thought. And to his delighted relief, he felt his feet rise from the dusty road.

"Rye!" gasped Sonia, gaping up at him.

"I thought — if the horsehair ring helps me run, and the serpent scale helps me swim, why should the feather not help me fly?" Rye laughed uncertainly. He still could not quite believe it.

And later, when he, Sonia, Dirk, and Faene were all linked together and floating over the forbidden forest like leaves blown in the wind, he still had his doubts.

The feather made them lighter than air, certainly, but being weightless was not the same as flying like a bird. It was very hard to move in any particular direction.

Rye quickly found that the only way was to trail awkwardly through the treetops, catching hold of each tree as he reached it and using it to propel him on to the next.

Twigs kept brushing the concealing hood from his head, and after a while, he stopped trying to keep it on. He had to keep his mind focused on what he was doing. He had discovered that the moment his thoughts wandered, he would start to drift off course.

Clumsy as it was, their progress was swift. At first, Rye used the stream, glinting below him, as a guide. Then Sonia called out, pointing down, and through a gap in the leaves he made out the narrow, winding path that he knew led up to the place where their journey had begun.

Yet still he could see no sign of the Wall of Weld looming ahead. He told himself the Wall must be concealed by ancient magic. He forced himself not to think about what would happen if they could not find the golden Door by sunset.

Instead, he concentrated on following the path. Now and again, he caught sight of a thick, slimy web sagging between two tree trunks, and knew a fell-dragon must be lurking nearby, waiting for prey. He saw the shadowy shapes of other creatures, too, scuttling or sliding in the undergrowth. He had no idea what they were, but was heartily glad to be floating above them, however awkwardly, instead of hurrying fearfully past their hiding places.

There were no Fellan to be seen, but he knew they were below, and aware of him. Their voices were whispering at the edges of his mind. He refused to let the whispers trouble him — refused to try to make out the words. He gripped the feather more tightly and kept his eyes on the path.

"Rye, take us down!" Sonia said suddenly. "The scarf I left as a marker is below!"

"It is not time to land yet!" Dirk protested. "The Wall is not in sight."

But Rye had learned that Sonia's instincts were to be trusted in matters such as this. He forced himself to think of settling to earth and at last managed to half clamber, half drift down to the forest floor, with his companions trailing behind him.

He dropped knee-deep into the thick carpet of dead leaves he so well remembered. Pushing the feather back into the bag, he looked around warily. There were the countless trunks of giant trees. There were the great rocks, the dense undergrowth.

And there was Sonia's red scarf, still knotted to a straggly bush.

The back of Rye's neck prickled with the feeling that he was being watched. He pulled the bell tree stick from his belt. It was not much of a weapon, and he wished fervently that Dirk still carried the skimmer hook. He could see no fell-dragons, but his mind was full of whispering voices.

The nine powers . . .

Edelle said too much. The treaty . . .

Have faith.

Sonia darted to the red scarf and began to free it.

"This is foolish," Dirk growled, holding Faene close to him. "You should have waited till the Door was in view."

Sonia swung around, tying the scarf loosely around her neck. "The Door *is* in view!" she snapped. "Where are your eyes?"

She marched past Rye, toward a towering sheet of rock half shrouded by overgrown bushes. And suddenly, like a shape emerging from a mist, a shimmering golden Door became visible in the rock's craggy brown surface.

Dirk and Faene gaped in amazement for a split second, then ran to the place. Rye stayed where he was, staring at the Door. There was something different about it, but he could not think what it was till Sonia spoke.

"There is no knob on this side," she said in a strangely flat voice. "I had not noticed that before."

"It is to keep unwanted visitors out, I daresay," said Dirk. "Stand aside." He put his right hand to the glinting carved surface and pushed.

Nothing happened. Cursing under his breath, Dirk pushed again, this time with both hands and as hard as he could, but still the Door did not move.

"Why does it not open?" Faene cried in panic.

"There must be a trick to it," Dirk panted, running his fingers rapidly over the carving, trying to find a secret trigger. "Or perhaps . . . yes, of course! I have been declared dead! The Door no longer recognizes me!"

He looked over his shoulder. "Rye! Come and —"

His eyes widened in horror. He was staring beyond Rye, at something behind Rye's back.

Rye's stomach lurched. He looked around. Only a few paces away, a giant, mottled shape was peeling from the trunk of a tree. The fell-dragon dropped to the ground and raised itself on its hind legs. Its dripping jaws opened, and it seemed to grin.

Only then, with the cries of Dirk, Sonia, and Faene ringing in his ears, did Rye remember that he was not wearing the concealing hood. Quick as a thought, he reached up and pulled the silk over his head.

The monstrous lizard hesitated. Then it seemed to decide that a being who could vanish before its eyes was not worth pursuing. It dropped to all fours again and prowled toward Sonia, Dirk, and Faene.

Rye lunged forward. All he could think of was reaching his companions, to share the hood with them. Never had he moved so fast. In a blink, the bell tree stick was clanging musically on golden carving as his hands slammed against the Door.

And the Door moved. The Door moved beneath his hands. He heard a soft creaking sound. . . .

"It is opening!" he yelled. "Hold on to me!"

He felt hands grip him. He saw a long, widening strip of blinding white light. He heard the fell-dragon bellow in baffled rage. Then he was jerked off his feet, and he, Sonia, Dirk, and Faene were swept together through the Door.

A FRIEND IN HIGH PLACES

They were in the Chamber of the Doors. Rye knew that, even with his eyes screwed shut. The smells of ash and ancient rock were very familiar. His skin was prickling with old magic.

Safe. Rye opened his eyes and gazed at the stone walls, the gaping fireplace, the dusty rock floor. The room looked smaller than he remembered. He felt his companions slipping away from him, but he could not move. For a moment, he could do nothing but stand motionless, gripped by the memory of the last time he had been in this place.

It had only been a few days ago, but it seemed like weeks — months! He felt like a different person from the boy who had recklessly lied his way into this secret chamber in the foundations of the Keep of Weld.

Slowly he turned to look behind him.

There were the three magic Doors, side by side. Magnificent gold, elegant silver, sturdy wood bound with brass.

Only a dead leaf on the floor showed that the golden Door had opened to let them in. No sound penetrated from the world outside.

Rye stared at the images carved into the Door's gleaming surface. On his first visit to the Chamber, he had thought they were just elaborate decorations. Now he could see that they were pictures of things that actually existed in the land beyond the Wall. Bloodhogs. Fell-dragons. Sea serpents . . .

He quickly turned away before his eyes could stray to the silver Door. He did not have to think about that yet. Not yet.

"Rye!" Sonia was kneeling by the fireplace. He went to her, aware that Dirk and Faene were slowly following him.

Sonia pointed into the shadows at the back of the fireplace, and, crouching, Rye saw the dangling end of a rope.

"The Keep chimneys are a maze, but if you keep hold of the rope, you will not get lost," Sonia said briskly. "It will be a tight squeeze for Dirk, but I daresay he can manage it, and Faene, too, if you use the feather to help them."

"You do not need help yourself, of course, Sonia?" Dirk inquired, trying but completely failing to hide his irritation.

"Oh no." Sonia laughed. "I am used to traveling by chimney, and I can climb like a clink." Pulling the red scarf over her mouth and nose to protect them from soot, she began recklessly tearing strips from the bottom of her already ragged skirt to make masks for her companions.

"But where will you take us, Sonia?" Faene asked anxiously. "If no one is to know —"

"One person must know," Sonia said, her voice muffled by the scarf.

"What?" Dirk frowned. "Who must know?"

"Let us just say that I have friends in high places," Sonia replied. "One friend, at least. Do not worry. She can be trusted."

❋

Even with the feather making them weightless, the climb up the dark chimney was not easy for Rye, Faene, and Dirk. Their elbows and knees scraped painfully against the stones as they half scrambled, half floated upward in an awkward chain.

Amid all his discomfort, Rye found himself feeling glad that Sonia, moving nimbly ahead of them in the gloom, was showing that she really could climb like a clink. He had never doubted it, but he was sure Dirk had suspected it was an idle boast. Now perhaps Dirk would see that idle boasting was not Sonia's way.

As they climbed higher, it became clear why Sonia had called the Keep chimneys a maze. The chimney they were using was obviously the oldest and largest, but it had many offshoots leading to fireplaces on other floors. By leaning into these offshoots, the climber could hear what was happening in the rooms beyond the fireplaces.

And so it was that, reaching the place where the Keep kitchen chimney joined the main stack, Rye suddenly heard, over the clatter of dishes, his mother's voice.

"I do not mind the task," Lisbeth was saying. "She always thanks me very politely."

"By the Wall, and so she should!" another woman retorted. "After you have toiled up all those stairs with a heavy tray!"

Bracing his back against the chimney wall, hissing a warning to Faene that he had stopped, Rye fumbled for the light crystal and pressed it against the blackened stones. A window appeared, and through it, he saw his mother in the room below.

Lisbeth was standing at a table chopping vegetables. An elderly woman was working with her, and a third woman was washing dishes on the other side of the room.

Like the other kitchen workers, Lisbeth was wearing a white apron and a white cap that covered her hair completely. She had deep shadows under her eyes and looked so pale that at first Rye feared she was ill. Then he saw that the old woman was just as pale, and realized that he had grown used to seeing faces browned by a stronger sun than Weld's.

"Well, I am very grateful you have taken over carrying the trays, my dear, and you are good to make light of it," the old woman said to Lisbeth. "I did it for years, but my poor knees would not have taken much more of it."

The third woman turned from the washing up. "It is a wicked waste of time and effort, I say," she said sharply. "Trays in her room three times a day indeed! If it is good enough for the Warden to eat in the dining room, why is it not good enough for his daughter?"

The old woman snorted. "If you had been here as long as I have, Bettina, you would know that the Warden likes his daughter to stay out of the way. The very sight of her makes him uncomfortable, they say, and he prefers other people not to see her either."

"What?" cried Lisbeth. "But why —?"

"Well, she should have been a boy, shouldn't she?" the old woman said, frowning over her chopping board. "The Warden wanted a son who could take his place as leader of Weld. He has no use for a daughter."

"Poor child," Lisbeth said in a low voice. And Rye, remembering the proud, closed face of the finely dressed young woman he had seen by chance on his first visit to the Keep, suddenly found that he was sharing his mother's pity for the Warden's daughter.

Bettina sniffed and went back to her washing up.

"The girl's mother, rest her sweet soul, died when the child was only toddling," Lisbeth's companion went on. "And the Warden could never make up his mind to marry again, so there have been no more children."

"The Warden can never make up his mind to do anything," grumbled the woman at the sink.

"My sons used to say that," Lisbeth murmured. "The two . . . who went beyond the Wall."

She raised her hand to the bib of her apron. Rye guessed that the two flower badges she had been sent when Dirk and Sholto were officially declared lost were pinned to her dress beneath the crisp white cloth.

"Do not grieve, my dear," the old woman muttered to her. "At least you know that your youngest is safe in the Center."

"Yes." Lisbeth nodded, trying to smile. "We may not be together, but Rye at least is safe."

Rye's heart seemed to twist in his chest.

"Rye!" Dirk called from below. "Move on, I beg you! I am stifling!"

And Rye, realizing that his brother had not heard their mother's voice, and knowing there was nothing to be done, pulled the crystal from the chimney wall and let the magic feather draw him on.

The next time he heard voices floating up through a chimney offshoot, he almost did not stop. Then a familiar name came to his ears and he halted abruptly.

"Tallus, Warden," a gruff voice repeated. "The Southwall healer. An elderly man, with a limp."

"Oh yes. Tallus. And what does the old nuisance want this time?"

Rye would have known the Warden's thin, irritable tones anywhere. Quickly he felt for the light crystal again.

"He says he must see you, sir," the gruff voice said. "He claims to have made an important discovery about the skimmers."

Rye pressed the crystal to the chimney wall. Again, it was as if a window had opened in the sooty stone.

He found himself looking down into a room he recognized. It was the waiting room where just a few days ago he had signed the statement all volunteers had to sign before going through the Wall.

He could see the tops of two heads by the polished table he so well remembered. One head was almost bald. It belonged, Rye was sure, to the officer who dealt with the volunteers. The other head, the Warden's, was engulfed in a large three-cornered red hat from which sprang a forest of nodding white plumes.

"I cannot see anyone now, Jordan," the Warden said fretfully. "I have two sympathy scrolls to sign and must review the changing of the guard very soon. Then there are the evening protection spells to be seen to. And then it will be time for dinner. Tell the old busybody to go away. I will meet with him another day. Possibly. If I have the time."

The bald man shook his head. "He says he will not leave the Keep until he has seen you, sir. He is sitting on the ground outside my office, telling his tale to anyone who will listen. And people *are* listening to him, sir, unfortunately. Is it your wish that I have him removed by force?"

"*Force?* Ah . . . well, now, yes, perhaps . . ."

"Only, he will not go quietly, sir, for sure," Jordan went on. "And he being so old and limping as well, it might not look good to the crowd."

"No indeed! By the Wall, what a dilemma!" The Warden wrung his pudgy little hands, then raised them to his hat as if to ensure that it was still securely in place. "Perhaps . . . ah . . ."

"Perhaps I should offer him a meal and a bed for the night, and say you will see him in the morning, sir," Jordan suggested smoothly.

"Yes!" The Warden's plumes swayed madly as he nodded with obvious relief. "That will get him out of the public view for now, at least. See to it, Jordan. At once!"

Rye tucked away the crystal and moved on up the chimney, burning to tell Dirk and Sonia what he had seen.

What had brought Tallus to the Keep? Surely he was not going to try yet again to persuade the Warden to put Sholto's skimmer repellent into use throughout the city? That idea had been rejected several times already. The Warden flatly refused to admit that a repellent might work where his spells of protection did not.

No, thought Rye. *It must be something else — something Tallus has discovered since I saw him, too, for he said nothing of it to me.*

At that moment, he realized that he could no longer hear the faint sounds of Sonia climbing ahead. No doubt she had grown tired of waiting for him and had hurried on to warn her mysterious "friend in high places" that she was bringing visitors.

Rye raised the red feather above his head, thought of flying, and heard Faene and Dirk gasp as he shot upward, faster than ever before.

In no time at all, he heard Sonia's voice calling him. There she was, a dark figure beckoning in the pale light that leaked into the chimney from yet another fireplace.

"Here, Rye!" she called. "I have told her. She is waiting to meet you."

Rye reached her and felt her hand touch his. With a low call of warning to Faene and Dirk, he twisted, crouched, and followed Sonia through the fireplace, crawling clumsily into the room beyond.

He fell onto a soft hearthrug and jumped to his feet, blinking in the sudden brightness. Paintings, tapestries, and bookshelves lined the curved walls of the room. A huge diamond-shaped window with hundreds of shining panes looked out on the pale Weld sky.

Rye realized with a shock that he was in the Keep tower. As his eyes adjusted to the light, as Faene and

Dirk clambered out of the fireplace after him, filthy and gasping, he saw a table on which lay an open drawing book, several fine brushes, and pots of colored ink. He saw curtained doorways that no doubt led into other rooms. He saw a golden harp and a book of music on a stand.

And he saw, standing beside the harp, rigid with disapproval, a dark-haired, finely dressed young woman.

Rye's jaw dropped as he recognized her.

It was the Warden's daughter.

THE TOWER

Thunderstruck, Rye turned quickly to Sonia. Her expression was a strange mixture of nervousness and defiance. Her hair hung in tangled rats' tails around her face, and her clothes were little more than rags. The contrast between her and the elegant young woman standing stiffly by the harp was absurd, but Rye had no urge to smile.

He felt fearful, and deeply embarrassed.

According to the kitchen workers, the Warden's daughter led a lonely life. No doubt it had amused her to befriend an unruly Keep orphan who made a habit of scrambling through the chimney system and who could bring her gossip and news. But this did not mean that three rough strangers were welcome here, in her private space. And it certainly did not mean that she was willing to risk hiding them from her father.

"Nocki, this is Rye," Sonia chattered, pulling Rye forward. "He was the volunteer who took me through the Wall. Behind him are Faene D'Or and Rye's brother Dirk, whom we rescued on the other side."

As Faene and Dirk scrambled up, pulling the sooty masks from their faces, their hostess pressed her lips together and curtseyed, very briefly, with a rustle of silken skirts.

"Faene — Rye — Dirk —" Sonia went on in a high voice, "this is Annocki, the Warden's daughter."

Dirk swore under his breath. Faene snatched off her cap and raised her chin before returning Annocki's curtsey. No doubt she was telling herself that she was the daughter of chiefs of Fleet, and need not feel cowed by anyone, however she was dressed.

Annocki shook her head. "Oh, Sonia," she sighed. "What am I to do with you?"

And such was the rueful affection in her voice that Rye's feelings did an abrupt somersault, and he felt a flicker of hope.

"Just trust me, Nocki!" Sonia said breathlessly. "I know this is hard for you, but there was nothing else to be done. We need food, and a place to sleep tonight. Then Faene will have to stay here in hiding, while Dirk, Rye, and I go back —"

"Sonia!" Annocki cut in sharply.

Sonia fell silent, biting her lip. Rye met Dirk's eyes and quickly looked away again.

Annocki clasped her hands tightly and took a deep breath.

"Be still, Sonia, just for a moment," she went on in a calmer voice. "You have taken me completely by surprise. I have been very worried about you. I have hardly slept since you left. And now, suddenly, you come back, bringing three strangers with you, and —"

"Indeed, we did not mean to intrude on your privacy, lady," Faene broke in, bright color rising in her golden cheeks. "We had no idea Sonia was bringing us to you. Please do not trouble yourself — about me, at least. I am sure that Dirk can find me somewhere else to stay."

Annocki blinked at her, clearly unable to believe that this well-spoken young woman was one of the crude, cruel barbarians she had been taught to fear.

Then suddenly she seemed to pull herself together. She moved quickly forward and held out her hand to Faene.

"Forgive me," she said, suddenly sounding far more human. "I did not mean to seem unwelcoming. My quarrel is only with Sonia, and I have become used to speaking to her very freely. We began as mistress and maid —"

"Lady-in-waiting, if you please!" Sonia protested.

Annocki sighed. "Lady-in-waiting, then. But that was a long time ago, and now we are like sisters, despite the differences between us."

"Nocki has tried to civilize me, but I fear she has failed," Sonia said smugly.

"So we have noticed," Dirk muttered.

Faene hesitated, then put out her own hand and allowed Annocki to take it.

"I have known Sonia for days, not years," she said steadily, "but in that time she has been a true friend to me. I well understand what you have suffered, thinking you had lost her."

"I am sorry, Nocki — sorry you have been worried, I mean," Sonia put in. "But you knew I was determined to get through the Wall this time."

"Indeed." Annocki smiled wryly. "But I thought you would fail, as you have failed so often before. None of the other volunteers agreed to take you."

"No," Sonia said, with a resentful glance at Dirk, "but luckily Rye was different."

"Only because you blackmailed me," Rye retorted, feeling his face grow hot.

Sonia shrugged. "It had to be done. No one noticed that I was gone, did they, Nocki?"

Annocki shook her head. "As far as anyone knows, you have been here all along. I have tried my best to give that impression, and no one has challenged me."

No one would dare, Rye thought, looking sideways at the young woman's proud, closed face. Annocki was very tense, he could feel it, and she continually avoided her visitors' eyes. He wondered uneasily how far she could be trusted.

Dirk was plainly wondering the same thing. He was looking warily around the room, very much on the alert.

Everyone jumped as there was a blare of trumpets from somewhere below. In a flash, Dirk had darted to the window and was looking down. Faene and Rye hurried to join him.

"It is nothing — only the changing of the guard," Sonia said, raising her voice slightly as drums began to beat, making the panes of the window rattle. "It happens at this time every day."

In the courtyard below, Keep soldiers were marching in a complicated pattern, the white feathers on their helmets bobbing. To one side, a small, plump figure in a plumed hat sat stiffly on a bored-looking black horse laden with red and gold trappings.

Rye fidgeted. He knew that if he had seen this fine spectacle a few days ago, when he first came to the Keep, he would have found it very impressive. He would have gazed at it in awe, as the citizens ringing the courtyard were doing at this moment.

But his time beyond the Wall had changed him, it seemed. All he felt now was a vague distaste. From above, the scene was almost comical. The soldiers looked like windup toys. The Warden looked like a doll stuffed with straw — a doll in a silly hat.

"I had forgotten," Dirk muttered, his eyes hard as he stared down. "I saw this ceremony when I first came here. The soldiers train for it, I was told, every morning, six days a week. By the Wall, why do they bother? They might as well be folk dancing for all the good it does for Weld."

Rye glanced over his shoulder at Annocki. She was frowning, but whether this was because she resented Dirk's criticism or because she agreed with it, he could not tell.

Turning back to the window, he raised his eyes and looked over the courtyard to the city beyond. The view was strangely pale, as if it had been painted with inks that were too watery. Stubby trees dotted the edges of flat, straight roads. Squat little houses lined the roads as far as the eye could see, with frequent sad gaps, like missing teeth, where skimmers had struck.

Rye suddenly understood how Sonia could have once mistaken a goat shelter for a house in the land beyond the golden Door. Looking down from this high tower, everything looked hunched, dull, and small.

Everything except the Wall. A towering, brooding presence, the Wall rose into the hazy sky, dwarfing everything within it, spreading like giant wings from both sides of the Keep, and disappearing into the distance. Close beside it, raw and ugly, ran the trench from which the clay for new bricks was dug.

Workers wearing bright yellow harnesses swarmed over the lower half of the Wall. The safety ropes netting the sheer clay surface trailed one minute and tightened the next as the men went about their work, mending and replacing, thickening and smoothing, busy and diligent as bees.

Rye saw Faene rub the pane in front of her with her sleeve. She could not understand why everything looked so dim. She thought the window was clouded. Dirk was glancing at her uneasily. Perhaps he, too, was seeing his home with new eyes and wondering if Faene of Fleet would ever be truly happy shut away inside the Wall.

Very unsettled, Rye turned away. And it was then he realized that Sonia and Annocki were whispering furiously at each other behind his back.

"Sonia, you ask too much!" he heard Annocki hiss. "You cannot expect me to —"

"Do not fuss, Nocki!"

"*Fuss?* Sonia, you are impossible! Can you not consider my feelings for one moment? Put yourself in my position!"

And abruptly Rye remembered just what that position was. The Warden had promised his daughter's hand in marriage to any volunteer who succeeded in saving Weld. Annocki was to have no choice in the matter. She was just part of the prize.

How she must have loathed seeing the volunteers streaming into the Keep when the Warden's notices about the quest first went up all over the city. How she must have cringed to think that one of these men was to be her husband whether she liked it or not — and even if he did not want her.

She was no doubt sickened by the very sight of Rye and Dirk, let alone by the idea of helping them. And as for Faene, the barbarian beauty Dirk so plainly loved . . .

"It will not be for long, Nocki!" Sonia whispered. "Rye, Dirk, and I will leave again in the morning, and with luck I will be back very soon, to give you the best of news, and the Warden the shock of his life!"

Annocki shook her head. Her eyes were bleak.

"My good, brave friend, you are dreaming. If the Enemy sending the skimmers can be destroyed, surely it will be this Dirk, or someone like him, who will do it. Not you."

Sonia lifted her chin. "It will be me," she said. "I know it seems strange, but somehow I feel even more certain of that now. Rye and Dirk will be my witnesses — and perhaps their brother, Sholto, too. The Warden will not be able to deny me."

Her face seemed lit from within. Her eyes were glittering green.

And at that moment Rye realized at last what was driving Sonia to risk the perils of the world outside the Wall. It had nothing to do with gaining glory for herself. She was doing it for Annocki — to save Annocki from the selfish whims of the Warden once and for all.

"Have faith, Nocki," Sonia urged. "Just a little longer."

Annocki bowed her head. "I will try. But, Sonia, I fear for you! And it is not just because the land of the barbarians is so dangerous. It is . . . Oh, I do not know how to explain it! You have been away only a few days, but I feel a change in you."

"A change?" Sonia stared at her.

Annocki nodded. "I cannot put my finger on the difference. But you seem more . . . more *alive*, somehow." She shrugged in embarrassment. "It makes no sense."

"It does!" Sonia seized her friend's hands. "I *feel* more alive, Nocki. It is as if my blood has become richer and is running faster through my veins. I thought I was imagining it, but if you sense it, too . . ."

Annocki looked troubled. "I fear you thrive on danger, Sonia. And if that is so —"

"No." Sonia shook her head. "It is the *place*! Everything is so big and bright! The sky is huge, and as blue as — as that!"

She pointed to a little blue pottery horse on Annocki's worktable and laughed as her friend looked disbelieving.

"Truly!" she insisted. "You can *breathe* out there, Nocki!"

"You can die out there also, Sonia," Annocki said grimly.

Sonia paused, biting her lip. "Yes," she admitted. "But somehow . . . it is worth it."

Much later, long after the diamond window had been closely shuttered, Rye lay on a mass of cushions with Dirk by his side, trying to will himself to sleep.

He had bathed luxuriously in a great tub with taps that gushed streams of steaming water. The cushions were soft beneath him. Most important of all, his stomach was pleasantly full. Annocki had eaten little, and Faene had refused food and gone early to bed, but he, Sonia, and Dirk had picked the loaded dinner tray clean.

Sleep should have come easily, but Rye's mind would not rest. As soon as they were alone, Dirk had seized the chance to try to persuade him to stay in Weld on the morrow. Rye's determination had not been shaken, but he hated disagreeing with Dirk. The argument had unsettled him.

And that was not all.

How fantastic and unreal the stories of their adventures beyond the golden Door had seemed, when told to the Warden's daughter in this rich, closed room!

How confusing it was, to be back in Weld yet not to feel the old sense of home!

How hard it had been to hear his mother's quiet voice at the door when she came with the dinner tray, and not be able to call out to her, or see her face-to-face!

And most of all, how nightmarish it was to lie for the first time in days sweating and stifled in a hot, sealed room, listening to the hideous, flapping, scrabbling rush of skimmers flying in their thousands over the Wall of Weld.

THE DREAM

It was very late when at last Rye's thoughts began to drift and blend into confused dreams. Over and over again, he half woke, turned restlessly, and fell into another shallow sleep. And in the early hours of the morning, dreams became nightmare. . . .

Sholto was bathed in weird red light that drained all color from his gaunt face. His hair had been cut so it was nothing but black stubble coating his skull.

Skimmers were lunging at him, baring their needle teeth, flapping their pale, leathery wings, slashing with the vicious spurs on their hind legs so that drops of venom, gleaming red as blood in the scarlet light, filled the air around them.

Yet Sholto did not move. He merely watched the frenzied beasts intently, his dark, clever eyes dropping now and then to the notebook in his hand. And somehow the creatures never reached him. They just lunged and lunged again, falling back repeatedly as if repelled by an invisible barrier.

But Sholto was in danger. Terrible danger. There was danger in the red light. There was danger in the shadows. Danger and horror, coming closer . . .

A clanking thud broke into the nightmare, and Rye woke, his heart pounding.

It was a dream, he told himself. *Only a dream.*

But his dreams of Dirk had been visions — glimpses of what Dirk had really been doing. And that meant . . .

A low moan escaped his lips. Beside him, Dirk sighed, mumbled, and turned over.

"Sorry, Rye," Sonia's voice whispered.

Rye's eyes flew open. It was very dark in the hot, close room, but gradually he made out a shape looming over him.

"I am sorry I woke you," Sonia murmured in the darkness. "Skimmers are attacking the chimney. There is no danger — the chimney is well sealed at the top in summer — but the sound startled me, and I dropped the sack of supplies."

"W-what?" Still half gripped by the nightmare, Rye sat up.

"I have been down to the kitchens to collect food for our journey," Sonia whispered. "The early hours are the best time for thieving. I have — Rye, what is wrong? You are shaking!"

"I had a fearful dream," Rye said thickly. "One

of the dreams that are — real. I saw Sholto . . . and skimmers."

"Skimmers?" Sonia hissed, dropping to her knees beside him. "Where? Did you see the place?"

"Red — it was all red," Rye muttered, trying to control his ragged breathing. "And something was coming — something worse than skimmers. A shadow. Cold . . . powerful . . . evil . . ."

He pressed his hands over his eyes. His teeth were chattering. He hated showing such weakness in front of Sonia, but he could not help it.

There was a pause, and then he felt Sonia touch his quaking arm.

"At least, however terrible it was, the dream proves that Sholto is still alive," she said quietly. "It also proves he chose the right Door."

"Yes." Rye took a deep, shuddering breath.

"And tomorrow we will set out to find him," said Sonia. "So put the dream out of your mind now and get some rest, Rye. That is what I am going to do. The waking bell will ring all too soon as it is."

She pressed his arm and retreated, dragging a sack that chinked and rattled as it rasped over the carpet to the bedroom door.

Strangely comforted, Rye settled back on his cushions. For a while, he kept his eyes open, afraid that if he slept again the vision of the red place would return to torment him. Then, deliberately, he made himself relax.

Sonia was right. However frightening it had been, the dream had proved that Sholto lived. That was a step forward. And tomorrow . . .

✳

Rye swam up from a sleep fathoms deep and sat up, blinking in the dimness. The shutter still covered the diamond window, blocking out the morning light and dulling the sound of the waking bell clanging in the courtyard far below. He could hear Sonia, Annocki, and Faene murmuring sleepily in their room, and Dirk yawning beside him.

But he could hear something else, too. Someone was knocking on the tower room door.

Sonia came bounding out of the bedroom and ran to the door. She was wearing a long red nightgown. Her coppery hair flew wildly around her shoulders.

"Yes?" she said sharply.

"Message from the Warden, ma'am!" a small, frightened voice piped.

"Push it under the door, if you please."

A large white envelope slid onto the carpet. Sonia bent and picked it up. "Thank you," she called.

"I — I am sure you would do the same for me!" gabbled the small voice, and footsteps went pattering away.

"Keep orphan," Sonia said curtly, turning away from the door. "How useful the Warden finds it to have a good supply of little messengers and be praised for his kindness in keeping them, too!"

Annocki and Faene had appeared in the bedroom doorway by now. Their eyes were puffy with sleep, but they had both taken the time to throw robes over their nightgowns.

"Shall I open it?" Sonia asked, holding up the envelope.

"Of course." Annocki frowned and drew her robe more closely around her chest as if she was cold.

"Make haste!" Dirk urged. Plainly he feared that somehow the Warden had found out that there were strangers in the Keep.

Sonia tore open the envelope, glanced at the message inside, hissed, and thrust the paper at Rye. With an embarrassed glance at Annocki, who nodded stiffly, Rye read the note aloud:

> *There was slight skimmer damage to the tower chimney last night. This damage must be repaired without delay. The Keep must be in perfect order at all times, especially in those areas that are visible to the public.*
>
> *Workers will be in the chimney above your sitting room throughout the day. I trust that you and your maid will not distract them from their duties.*
>
> *The Warden of Weld*

Rye could not believe it — he could not believe a father could write to his daughter so coldly! He looked up. There were dark red patches on Annocki's cheekbones. Her dark eyes were burning with anger.

Faene was clearly very shocked. No doubt she wondered what sort of place she had come to, where parents and children could be so at odds. She turned to Dirk for reassurance, but Dirk's mind was on other things. He was glaring at the fireplace.

Soot had begun drifting down onto the hearth. There were muffled voices from above, and a wrenching, tearing sound as the chimney block was removed. The Warden's orders were being obeyed promptly, it seemed.

"By the Wall, this is criminal!" Dirk burst out. "What of all the homes destroyed last night? How does the Warden dare to waste a single worker on his cursed chimney?"

"Hush, Dirk!" Faene whispered, hurrying to his side and glancing nervously at Annocki.

"Nothing the Warden does surprises me!" snapped Sonia. "But it is a great nuisance. Do you not see? While workers are in the chimney up here, we cannot use it! They will spy us climbing down, and the Warden is sure to hear of it."

"Then we are trapped here all day." Rye felt sick. Memories of the dream flooded his mind, rising like a sour tide.

"No!" Sonia pressed her lips together and shook her head. "This is the safest and most convenient way to the Chamber of the Doors, certainly. But there is more than one fireplace in the Keep. The one in the waiting room on the ground floor would be the best, I think. The workers will not be able to see us down there. We will try our luck straight after breakfast."

"Sonia . . ." Annocki began warningly.

Sonia took not the slightest notice. She smiled at Rye and Dirk.

"Do not worry," she said. "All we have to do is take a risk — and by now, we should be used to that."

✻

An hour later, his hand on Sonia's shoulder and Dirk's hand heavy on his back, Rye was creeping down the narrow, winding steps that led directly from the tower to the ground floor of the Keep. The concealing hood was on his head, and the speed ring was on his finger. The bell tree stick was in his belt, and a bundle containing food and water was slung on his back. He felt as if a thousand butterflies were fluttering in his stomach.

"We are nearly at the bottom," Sonia warned softly. "Be ready."

Rye tightened his grip on her shoulder as she began to move a little faster.

This morning, Sonia looked very much as she had when he had first met her. Despite Annocki's protests, she had again put on the red cap, tunic, and trousers of a Keep orphan. The red scarf, washed and dried overnight, was knotted around her throat. As before, she carried her own small bundle of supplies at her waist, tied in place with the old plaited rope belt she had kept with her throughout the journey beyond the golden Door.

Rye could feel her tension and excitement. It seemed to run through his fingers, like the tingle he felt when he touched the little bag of powers hanging around his neck. Despite everything that had happened to her beyond the Wall the last time, Sonia could hardly wait to escape from Weld again.

Perhaps Annocki was right, and Sonia thrived on danger. The idea had plainly returned to Annocki's mind when she had said good-bye at the tower room door. Her face had been very sober as she hugged Sonia, earnestly begging her to take care.

"Do not worry, Nocki!" Sonia had said, returning the hug warmly. "I will be back. And in the meantime, you will have Faene to keep you company."

"Faene does not seem to want company at present," Annocki replied dryly, glancing over her shoulder. After tearfully farewelling Dirk, Faene had retreated to the bedroom and had not shown her face since.

"Oh, she will soon recover," said Sonia, with what Rye thought was quite mistaken assurance. "Or she will pretend to. Faene's manners are far better than mine."

"That would not be difficult," Annocki had snapped. But her smile had taken the sting from her words, and she had stood watching Sonia, Rye, and Dirk until they were out of sight.

"There!" Rye heard Sonia whisper.

Light shone dimly through an archway not far below. A few more steps, and they could see through the archway to a broad, stone-paved hallway lined with doors. People were hurrying up and down the hall — Keep workers with brooms and mops, officials carrying scrolls and folders, scurrying Keep orphans.

They all looked busy, intent on their morning duties. But there was no jostling, and there were certainly no collisions, because in the polite Weld way, everyone was keeping well to the right.

Following their plan, Rye, Dirk, and Sonia waited for a gap in the crowd passing the archway, then stepped smartly across to the middle of the hall where no one was walking at all.

People streamed along on either side of them, following the shallow paths that had been worn in the ancient floor by thousands of feet over the centuries. Rye wondered if anyone except cleaners had ever actually trodden on the stones where he and his companions now stood. Did the Warden ever stroll down the middle of the hall when he was alone, for example? Just to show he could?

The thought made Rye smile. The fluttering in his stomach eased.

"This way!" Sonia whispered, jerking her head to the left.

Hands tightly linked, they began to walk. The hall's central strip stretched ahead of them, wide and bare as a private road. It came to Rye that nothing he had done so far — even lying to the Warden — had made him feel quite so keenly that he had stepped outside the normal life of Weld.

"There," Sonia breathed, pointing to an open doorway on the right. "Be very quiet. There will be soldiers on guard inside."

They waited for a break in the passing crowd, then dashed through the doorway into a grand sitting room furnished with armchairs, sofas, and low tables.

Despite Sonia's warning, the room was deserted. Tall double doors stood open at one end, and through the gap Rye could see women in white aprons clearing a long dining table. Two soldiers stood by the head of the table, chatting to the women and finishing off a platter of cold sausages.

"Those men are supposed to be on guard in here," Sonia breathed. "What a piece of luck!"

She led the way to a door at the opposite end of the room and cautiously turned the gleaming knob. The door eased open with only the tiniest of creaks, and Rye and Dirk followed her into the room beyond.

The waiting room looked exactly as Rye remembered it. There was the fireplace, its hearth lightly sprinkled with soot. There were the chairs arranged around the walls, the long red curtains, and the polished table with its inkwell and the carved box in which all the Volunteer Statements were kept.

"Good!" Sonia sighed with relief. "From here it should be easy."

"Who is that?" a cracked voice cried from a dim corner.

As Rye, Dirk, and Sonia froze, a small, crabbed figure jumped up and limped forward, scowling ferociously.

THE DOORS

With a shock, Rye recognized Tallus the healer. The events of the night before had made him forget completely that Sholto's old master was at the Keep.

Tallus was wearing a rubbed green velvet coat, brightly checked trousers, enormous walking boots, and an ancient black broad-brimmed hat. These garments — the healer's traveling costume, no doubt — made him look strange enough. But the really odd thing about his appearance was the large hand-lettered sign stuck into the hat's band.

We can FIGHT the SKIMMERS!!! ASK ME HOW!!!

"Show yourselves!" Tallus shouted, shaking his fist. "I know you are there!"

The door on the other side of the room flew open, and the Warden rushed in, his pale eyes bulging, his scanty hair flopped limply over his forehead.

"What is the meaning of this uproar?" he demanded. "I am only a trifle late for our meeting, Master Tallus. There is no need to shout!"

"Aha!" cried Tallus, swinging around to confront him. "So, you have set spies on me, have you, Warden? I might have known!"

"S-spies?" spluttered the Warden. "What do you mean?"

"Someone came in!" Tallus roared. "I saw that door over there open and close! And then I heard a voice! Someone is hiding in here!"

He glared around the room. The Warden eyed him nervously, clearly wondering if soldiers should be called to subdue this madman. Rye, Dirk, and Sonia stood stock-still, not daring to move.

"Well, what does it matter?" snapped Tallus. "The more people who hear what I have to say, the better! Warden, I have developed an important theory regarding the skimmers. You must listen to me!"

"Yes, well, I am listening, Master Tallus," the Warden said peevishly. "But I am very pressed for time this morning, so —"

He broke off as Tallus held up a bony finger.

"I have been blind," the healer announced.

"Blind — ha, that is a good one! But a few days ago I saw it all in a flash."

"Did you, indeed?" the Warden muttered.

Tallus nodded. "I was examining a skimmer — a very fresh specimen, the best I have ever had. A young friend had called by just before I began. He wanted my advice about . . . about something that need not concern us here."

Rye felt a little jolt. Tallus was talking about him! For an instant, he was back in the healer's workroom. He was back with the steam and the smell. He could see the dead skimmer lying on the table, its goat-sized body covered in pale, velvety fuzz, its leathery wings outspread, its ratlike snout snarling. . . .

He shivered. He felt Dirk and Sonia glance at him curiously, but did not look at them.

"The boy mentioned the specimen's eyes," Tallus went on. "He had never seen a dead skimmer's eyes in such good condition before. The eyes are fragile and usually bleed you know, when —"

The Warden shuddered. "Spare me the details, if you please," he said. "I have just had breakfast."

Tallus snorted. "The point is, when my young friend had left, I looked at my specimen's eyes more closely. In all our research, my apprentice and I have paid little attention to the eyes —"

"Well, of course not!" the Warden broke in impatiently. "Skimmers are as good as blind, as I understand it."

"In daylight they are," said Tallus. "It has long been my theory, and my apprentice agrees with me, that skimmers live and breed in the dark — in a cavern underground, perhaps, where sight is not important."

Or in some foul place where the only light is dull red, thought Rye, feeling cold inside as he remembered his dream.

"They emerge at night to hunt," Tallus continued. "And why?"

The Warden stared at him. "Because they are hungry, of course! Really, Master Tallus, you must get to the —"

"No!" Tallus cried, his voice cracking. "Skimmers hunt at night because they *cannot* hunt during the day! Because daylight renders them helpless! It is their one weakness. When I looked closely at the specimen's eyes, I saw clearly that this must be so. The eyes were totally without protection. Almost transparent!"

"Yes, well, that is all very interesting," the Warden mumbled, looking queasy. "But —"

"And it suddenly came to me!" Tallus exclaimed. "It is so obvious, once you have seen it! Ever since the skimmer invasions began, Warden, we have been blanketing Weld in darkness at night. But we should have been doing the exact opposite!"

"The —?"

"We should have been repelling the beasts by using their one weakness against them! We should have been defending ourselves with *light*!"

"Light?" the Warden repeated, frowning. "Are you mad, Master Tallus? Light *attracts* the skimmers. How many of our more careless citizens, poor souls, have perished because —"

"Because a chink of light in a pool of darkness creates a target, and one small lantern is no real threat!" cried Tallus. "I am not talking about leaving a few house lights burning, Warden! My plan is to make the sky of Weld blaze, so night is as bright as day!"

The Warden's mouth fell open.

Tallus pulled a folded paper from one of his many pockets and shook it open. It was covered with diagrams and notes.

"I have worked it all out," he said, flattening the paper on the polished table and beckoning impatiently for the Warden to come and look. "Tall columns, higher than the rooftops, must be built all over the city —"

"Columns?" murmured the Warden, staring vacantly at the paper.

"At the top of each column we place a large lantern," Tallus rattled on, stabbing his finger at one of the diagrams. "We can use the Keep lanterns — they are the biggest we have, and you must have thousands of them here."

"The Keep lanterns?" the Warden repeated faintly.

Tallus nodded. "Each lantern will be surrounded by mirrors so that the light is spread and reflected upward. The Keep can supply the mirrors as well.

Every soldier has his own mirror, I hear, and there are many kept in stock."

"Yes, well, it is very important that the soldiers are always neatly —"

"Between them, the lanterns and mirrors should make enough light to repel the skimmers and force them to go elsewhere to feed," Tallus finished, slapping the paper triumphantly. "You see?"

He glanced at the Warden expectantly. The Warden frowned and rubbed his chin.

"Yes," he said slowly. "Well, Master Tallus, I will certainly give your suggestion some thought. . . ."

Sonia groaned. Rye stiffened, but luckily neither Tallus nor the Warden seemed to have heard her.

"Some *thought*?" Tallus yelled.

The Warden straightened his plump shoulders. "Possibly your idea has some merit, Master Tallus," he said carefully. "But before we clutter our tidy streets with ugly columns — not to mention removing vital equipment from the Keep — we must discuss the whole matter thoroughly. One thing you have not considered, for example, is who is going to build all these columns."

Tallus goggled at him. "But — obviously — the best people for the task would be the Wall workers! They would raise the columns in a matter of —"

"Out of the question!" the Warden exclaimed. "We cannot spare men from the Wall! The work is behind as it is!"

"But —" Tallus snatched off his hat in frustration, releasing his floss of wild, white hair. "But Warden, what is the point in using most of our workforce to strengthen the Wall when our attackers are flying *over* it?"

The Warden's face became almost pitying. "The Wall has been Weld's defense for a thousand years, since the time of its founder, the sorcerer Dann, Master Tallus," he murmured, as if instructing a small and rather stupid child. "It is my sacred trust, as it was my father's trust, and my grandfather's, and that of all of my family who came before them. Whatever else happens, our labors on the Wall must not be halted — not for a single working day."

"Then use the Keep soldiers to build the columns!" roared Tallus, tearing at his hair. "Bless the Wall, what else do they have to do but prance about practicing their marching and putting up signs?"

The Warden drew himself up. "You go too far, Master Tallus!" he said coldly. "This interview is at an end. Good morning!"

Picking up the skirts of his robe, he whisked huffily from the room without a backward glance.

Tallus dashed his hat to the floor and stamped on it.

"So now you know, spies!" he raged. "Now you know what a buffoon your Warden is! Well, if he will not listen to me, others will! Tell him that or not, as you like!"

He snatched up his crumpled hat, grabbed the paper from the polished table, and stormed out, slamming the door behind him.

"Well!" Rye said shakily.

"Make haste!" Sonia urged, hurrying toward the fireplace. "Before anyone else comes!"

In moments, they had wriggled up the chimney branch to the wider main stack, where Sonia's knotted rope still dangled from the blackness above. Rye pushed back the magic hood and tucked it beneath his collar to protect it from the soot.

"Was the old man right, do you think?" Sonia asked, her voice muffled by the scarf she had pulled over her mouth and nose. "*Would* bright light scare off the skimmers?"

"It makes sense," Dirk said.

"If only the Warden had agreed to try it," Rye sighed. "Just in a small part of Weld at first, perhaps, and then —"

Sonia snorted. "He was never going to agree. For one thing, it would mean admitting he has been wrong for all these years."

"And for another, he is terrified of anything new," Dirk added bitterly.

Rye shook his head in the gloom. He knew that Tallus was not going to abandon his idea just because the Warden would not cooperate with him. Tallus would try to act alone. And the Warden, angry and frightened, would see that as rebellion.

"There is going to be trouble," Dirk said, echoing his thoughts.

"Perhaps there is," Sonia answered grimly. "But we cannot be worried about that now. Come on."

Gripping the rope firmly, they began their downward journey.

Sonia moved quickly, with the ease of long practice. Dirk did almost as well. Rye gritted his teeth and tried to ignore the ache in his hands. When he heard dim clattering, he realized he was moving past the kitchen, but this time, he did not even think of stopping to catch a glimpse of his mother. And as he sank lower, a sense of ancient mystery enfolded him, making it hard to breathe or even to think.

Sonia and Dirk were waiting impatiently when at last he crawled out of the fireplace into the dim, echoing space that was the Chamber of the Doors. Sonia's face was taut with excitement as she grabbed his hand and turned him to face the three Doors.

On the left, the golden Door glowed against the rough stone of the wall. On the right stood the wooden Door, solid and strong. Between them, the silver Door gleamed coldly.

Rye made himself look at the strange patterns flowing across the silver surface. The longer he looked, the more he began to see, among the mysterious lines, the shapes of monstrous birds with long necks, cruel, curved beaks, and vast, outspread wings.

His skin crawled. A cold tide of dread swept

through him. Shuddering, he quickly raised his eyes to the rhyme carved in the stone above the Doors.

THREE MAGIC DOORS YOU HERE BEHOLD
TIME TO CHOOSE: WOOD? SILVER? GOLD?
LISTEN TO YOUR INNER VOICE
AND YOU WILL MAKE THE WISEST CHOICE.

The final lines whispered in Rye's mind like the soft, secret voices of the Fellan. He turned toward the wooden Door like a flower turning to face the sun. Barely conscious of what he was doing, he took a step forward, raising his hand.

"No, Rye!"

Rye stopped, very startled, as Sonia's voice cut through the feeling of longing that had almost overwhelmed him. He turned to look at her. There was an odd, strained expression on her face. Behind her, Dirk was looking aghast.

"You cannot choose for yourself, Rye," Sonia said. "Remember your dream. If we are to find the skimmers, we must follow Sholto through the silver Door."

Rye glared at her. She returned his gaze with a steady stare of her own, and abruptly his anger died, leaving confusion in its place.

"I — I am sorry," he stammered. "The wooden Door seemed to draw me. I felt the lure the first day I was here, but this time it was much stronger. I cannot explain. . . ."

Dirk looked confused, but Sonia's face softened. "There is no need to explain," she said. "I felt it, too."

As Rye stared at her, she smiled ruefully. "Perhaps one day you and I will be able to choose a Door for ourselves, Rye. When all this is over."

"Perhaps," Rye agreed, though he did not believe it. The skimmers and their evil master were at the end of this journey. Whether it ended in triumph or disaster for Rye, Dirk, and Sonia, it was unlikely that any of them would face the Doors a third time.

"You should use the hood, Rye," Sonia said, with a sudden return to briskness. "We have no idea what might be waiting for us outside."

Rye pulled up the hood. Sonia took his arm, and he took Dirk's. They moved to stand before the silver Door.

Rye reached out for the slender handle. The moment his fingers touched it, the Door began to open.

Again he saw a widening strip of blinding light. Again he felt an invisible power drawing him forward.

And again he was pulled off his feet, as the world of the silver Door dragged him in.

THE PYRAMID

R ye felt something tickling his closed eyelid. Just for a moment, he thought he was lying in the shade of the bell tree at home, and a falling leaf had drifted onto his face. Half smiling, he put up his hand to brush the leaf off, and felt movement beneath his fingers.

He yelled and sat up, slapping at his eye. Wings whirred frantically, and he caught a brief glimpse of something streaking away into the air.

He felt for his hood and found that it was still in place. So the flying creature, whatever it was, could not have seen him. It must have sensed him — felt his warmth, perhaps.

Sonia was crawling to her knees beside him. She was staring around blankly. A tangle of sticks was caught in her scarf, just below her ear, but she seemed unaware of it.

Then the tangle moved. Rye's stomach heaved as he realized that the sticks were legs and at the same moment saw stiff transparent wings, a head filled with glittering eyes, a needlelike stinger poised to strike. . . .

Sonia screamed as he shouted and lunged at her. Again there was the whir of wings, but this time, Rye saw the creature clearly as it sped away. It was shaped like the small blood-sucking insects called whines that plagued the people of Weld in warm, damp weather. But it was huge — as big as his fist!

Pushing back his hood, he scrambled to his feet, pulling Sonia up with him. She was deathly pale. With one hand she clung to Rye, with the other she brushed feverishly at her neck as if to make absolutely sure that the monstrous insect was no longer there.

"By the Wall, where are we?" Dirk grunted, crawling to his feet behind them.

"Wherever it is," Sonia said bleakly, "it is not Dorne."

Very startled, Rye tore his eyes from her stricken face and for the first time registered his surroundings.

He saw a barren wasteland of rounded, weirdly patterned stones and gaping holes from which oozed a sickly yellow mist. Thick gray cloud hung low overhead like a brooding ceiling, and walls of fog rose on every side, obscuring whatever was beyond.

The place was utterly desolate. There was not a single green, growing thing. There was not a breath of wind. And there was no sound at all.

Instinctively, Rye looked over his shoulder for the silver Door, but there was no sign of it — and no sign of the Wall of Weld either. He was not surprised, but still an iron hand seemed to clutch at his heart.

"Of course this is Dorne!" he retorted, more sharply than he had meant.

Sonia shook her head helplessly.

"We must be on the eastern side of the island," said Dirk, bending to examine something at his feet. "We were told that the east was wild and barren. People fled here to escape from Olt, Faene says, but before that, it was deserted. If this place is an example of one of its beauty spots, I can see why."

His small joke fell flat. Sonia's expression did not change.

"This cannot be Dorne," she repeated dully. "Everything here is dead."

Rye fought down a surge of irritation. "Well, there is no point in standing around arguing about it," he said. "The silver Door delivered us here, and that is all that counts. Which way do you think we should go?"

Sonia merely shrugged. Dirk, who had pried a strangely shaped object from the ground and was scraping it clean with the side of his boot, did not appear to be listening. And as Rye surveyed the dreary wasteland around him, his own will to move began to falter.

The place reeked of sadness and loss.

Everything here is dead. . . .

He glanced back at Sonia. She was gnawing her bottom lip. Her shoulders were drooping, her eyes dull as muddy water.

And suddenly he understood that he had begun to feel what she had been feeling all along. It was as if the weird rocks, the lowering sky, the despair that seemed to seep from the ravaged earth like the yellow mist, were somehow draining his strength. He could feel himself wilting where he stood, like a plant starved of water, like a flame starved of air.

What was happening? Could the mist be some kind of poison? Or could it be . . . ?

Sorcery!

Rye recalled the evil shadow of his dream and instinctively crossed his fingers and his wrists. Then, determined to resist the spell, he lurched forward.

Almost at once, he tripped and fell. His knees and the palms of his hands struck hard, lumpy ground. Scalding tears of pain sprang into his eyes.

What in Weld are you doing, Rye, barging about without a thought in your head?

Rye froze where he lay. The drawling voice in his mind was so clear that it was almost as if Sholto had actually spoken to him!

And in that moment he knew, without question, that Sholto had been in this very spot not so long ago. He jerked his head up, and through the tears that still blurred his eyes, he saw his brother standing in the distance among the patterned rocks, writing in a notebook.

His heart leaped, but just as he drew breath to call out, the lean, dark figure flickered and disappeared.

An illusion! Rye's throat tightened with bitter disappointment. But then he saw Sholto again. This time, Sholto was a little closer, peering intently into a hole in the earth as if trying to work out the yellow mist's cause. And no sooner had this second image vanished than another appeared, closer still and a little to Rye's left.

In this vision, Sholto had his sleeves rolled up, and his brow was gleaming with sweat. Two of the giant insects were circling him, but he was paying no attention to them. He was lifting stones, stolidly piling one upon the other like a child making a tower of toy bricks.

Rye blinked, and again Sholto's figure vanished. But something remained where it had been — a small pyramid of stones, its peak rising just a little above the surrounding rocks.

Rye gaped at it, awestruck. If he had not seen Sholto building this marker, he would probably not have noticed it among all the other piles of rocks that littered the ground. Even if he had come across it by chance, he might not have realized it was made by human hands.

But there it stood, clear evidence that he had seen the past — seen Sholto in the past! The visions had been as true as the glimpses of Sholto that had so often come to him in dreams.

Or . . . was the pyramid itself an illusion?

Rye had to know. Calling hoarsely to the others, he jumped up and began scrambling across the rocks.

He reached the pyramid in moments. It stood in a small circle of cleared earth and was almost as tall as he was. He put out his hands and touched it. It was solid. It was real.

So Sholto had truly been here, and Sholto had survived — survived to make his way to the red place, to find the source of the skimmers.

And if he could do it, we can do it, too, Rye thought. Deliberately he breathed out, letting the last of his fear and tension go.

"What is it?" Sonia asked fretfully, coming up behind him. Rye glanced at her over his shoulder. She still looked listless, but at least she had followed him.

"Sholto built this," he said. "I saw him doing it."

Her eyes widened, but before she could ask what he meant, he turned back to the pyramid. And it was only then that he realized why the rocks looked so oddly rounded and were so strangely patterned.

Every stone was completely covered in snails! The creatures' shells, striped and dotted with black, brown, orange, pink, and blue, were pressed as closely together as tiles on a richly decorated wall.

Amazed that he had not realized this before, Rye prodded the nearest snails with the tip of one finger. He could not shift them. They were clearly very much alive, holding on for dear life.

They were similar to the sea snails Rye had seen clustered on the piers of the fishermen's jetty in Oltan bay. These were land creatures, though, and the colors of their shells were not so bright.

But just because of that, they reminded him of something else.

Wondering, he slid his fingers into the little bag hanging around his neck. He found the smooth, round object he was seeking and drew it out.

The snail shell looked faded in the dull light. Rye put it into the palm of his hand and examined it.

There was no doubt. Except that it was empty and lifeless, it was exactly like the millions of shells that now surrounded him.

"Sonia!" Rye said slowly. "We *are* in Dorne — here is the proof of it!"

Sonia leaned forward and looked from the shell in his hand to the snails studding the pyramid.

"What does this mean?" she whispered, with more excitement in her voice than Rye had heard since they went through the silver Door.

Rye hesitated. "If it is like the feather, the ring, and the serpent scale, the shell's power has something to do with the creature it came from," he said at last. "Perhaps it will help us to hide."

"The hood does that already," Sonia objected, turning back to the pyramid and scanning the living snails eagerly. "It must be . . . Oh! What is that?"

She crouched and pointed at something white that was poking through a small gap in the pyramid's base. Gingerly she pulled at the thing, and it came away in her hand. It was a scrap of paper, its edges nibbled to lace by snails.

Rye's heart thudded as he recognized the writing on the fragment.

"Sholto!" he breathed. He swung around to call Dirk, saw that Dirk was still busy with whatever he had found on the ground, and quickly looked back to read the scrap in Sonia's hand.

> 2 fresh specimens this morn. Wings v.
> frayed—extreme old age. Eyes burned.
> Wounds suggest collision tree / rock.
> Theory holds: Too slow reaching shelter
> before sunrise & killed while flying blind.
> Still no sign of nest but

"He found dead skimmers," Rye muttered. "Look on the other side." Sonia turned the paper over, and sure enough there were more words on the back.

> & barely escaped with my life. Sealed cave
> & managed a few hours' sleep. Rain pots
> almost full this morn. so could wash &
> shave. Still cannot shake feeling I am being
> watched. Lack of sleep, possibly, or perhaps

Sonia shook her head in confusion.

"It is from Sholto's notebook," Rye said, battling the fear that had chilled him the moment he saw the paper. "But he would not have torn a page out. I do not know why it is here."

Then, suddenly, he did know. Ignoring Sonia's exclamations, he thrust the magic snail shell into his pocket and began pulling stones from the top of the pyramid. As he had expected, the structure was hollow.

He peered inside and found that the cavity contained some tatters of oiled cloth, the broken pieces of a clay pot, some lumps of candle wax, and the remains of a small book.

The book's covers had been eaten away. Most of its pages had been reduced to flakes of paper clinging to a threadbare spine. The few scattered fragments that had survived had been chewed almost to pieces. Rye gathered them carefully and showed them to Sonia with a rueful shrug.

"It looks as if Sholto filled an entire notebook in this place and hid it when he moved on," he said, sliding the fragile scraps into his pocket to keep them safe. "He wrapped the book in oiled cloth and put it into a pot sealed with wax. No doubt he thought that was protection enough from the snails. But it was not. These snails are not like the snails that prey on the vegetable fields of Weld. They will eat anything, it seems, even wax and clay."

"Perhaps that is their power," Sonia joked feebly. "Perhaps whenever you hold the shell, Rye, you will be able to eat clay, too."

Rye smiled, though in truth he did not feel like it. He retrieved the little snail shell from among the paper fragments in his pocket and weighed it thoughtfully in his palm.

"*Rye!*"

Rye and Sonia jumped violently as the shout rang out. Dirk was hurrying awkwardly toward them, sliding and stumbling on the rocks. He was brandishing a dingy skimmer hook.

That must have been what he found on the ground, Rye thought in confusion. *But why is he —?*

"Rye! Behind you!" Dirk roared, his finger stabbing at the sky. "Put on the hood! The hood!"

Rye spun around. Sonia was looking up, her face rigid with fear.

A terrifying form was sweeping down through the cloud. It was a gigantic bird, a bird as big as a Weld house, with vast wings and a long, twisting neck that was spiked like the neck of a sea serpent.

It was the monstrous bird of which Rye had once dreamed — the bird pictured on the silver Door.

DISCOVERIES

The giant bird opened its cruel hooked beak and screeched. The sound echoed from the rocks, harsh, hideous, pitiless. Rye pulled the hood over his head and seized Sonia's arm, but the monster faltered only for a split second before flying on.

Now they could hear the sound of its wings, pounding the air like waves crashing on the shore. It was heading straight for them, its razor-sharp talons spread wide, ready to seize, to slash. . . .

"It can still see us!" Rye shouted. "The hood does not —"

A shadow loomed over them. They rocked in the gale of the bird's mighty wing beats. The air filled with a vile, bitter stench.

In terror, they threw themselves down, covering their heads with their arms. There was the thud of running feet and the sound of laboring breaths, and the next moment, a heavy body was rolling on top of them, pressing them hard against the pyramid.

"Stay still!" Dirk panted. "I will try to beat the creature back. I have a skimmer hook —"

"Throw it away!" Sonia screamed. "The metal will affect the magic of the hood!"

"The magic is affected already!" Dirk roared back. "I could see you — only faintly, but enough! This weapon is our only chance! By a miracle, I spied it lying among the rocks. One of the Wall worker volunteers who chose the silver Door must have come to grief —"

His voice was lost in a tumult of sound. Suddenly the monster's wing beats were like thunder above them, blasting them with a freezing, stinking gale that seemed thick with malice. And at that moment, Rye was swept by the knowledge that this beast was no mere hunter of the air. It was an evil, unnatural thing, a creature of the dark power he had sensed in his dream.

He felt Dirk struggling to resist the wind, to wield the great hook, and knew it was hopeless. In despair, he heard Dirk's curse and a dull clang, and guessed that the weapon had been swept from his brother's hand.

Then the bird was upon them. With sharp cracking sounds, the terrible beak snapped shut once, twice, three times. Talons rasped on stone again and again. A long, grating screech split the air.

Rye lay locked in a daze of horror, feeling Sonia quaking beside him, waiting for the cry of agony that would tell him Dirk had been taken, waiting for the monster's talons to rake his own back.

But it did not happen. The sounds continued, the moments passed . . . and it did not happen.

And then, abruptly, the deafening screeches and the sounds of attacking beak and talons ceased. The pounding of giant wings began again. Again a great wind beat down on the rocks. Then the gale became less, and the pounding grew fainter. And at last, there was silence.

Rye felt Dirk roll away from him. Hardly daring to believe that the ordeal was over, he sat up, blinking.

Dirk was tugging at the skimmer hook, which had landed some distance away and was jammed between two rocks. The monstrous bird was flying back the way it had come. As Rye watched, it wheeled to the left, and for a split second, he saw its hideous shape silhouetted against the gray sky. Then it soared into the cloud, and was gone.

"What happened?" he asked blankly. "Why did it stop attacking us?"

"It has gone, that is all I care about," Sonia groaned, climbing painfully to her feet. "Oh, I am bruised all over!"

"Be grateful you were not torn to pieces," Dirk growled, striding back to them with the great hook in his hand. "By the Wall, Rye, do you not see now how insane it was for you and the girl to come here? You must go back!"

"We arrived knowing that this place must be dangerous," Sonia replied coldly. "And as for going back . . . Rye is free to do as he likes, but I have no intention of letting you beat me to the source of the skimmers, Dirk."

"You little fool!" shouted Dirk. "You have no chance whatever of destroying the Enemy! All you will do is hamper me, and in the end get us all killed! Why, what happened just now is proof of that! If it had not been for me —"

Sonia tossed her head. "You did nothing just now as far as I can see, you big oaf, but fall on top of us and bruise us black-and-blue! The bird —"

"Stop it!" Rye yelled at the top of his voice.

Startled, Sonia and Dirk both turned to stare at him. He scrambled to his feet and gestured furiously at the surrounding rocks and what remained of the pyramid. Great grooves had been carved into the stones. Thousands of snails torn away by the monster's talons were lying in heaps on the ground.

"Are you both mad, fighting like — like a pair of ducks squabbling over a worm?" Rye stormed. "We must think! Why did the bird go, when it could have killed us easily? What made it give up?"

"Well . . . the hood," Sonia said, eyeing him uncertainly. "The bird could not see us clearly. It was just lucky that your brother's stupid hook was blown —"

"It was not the hood!" Rye broke in, clenching his fists. "The creature might not have been able to see us clearly, but it could see us well enough to swoop down here, right here, and attack! We heard the sounds of its beak and talons! Why did they not injure us? Why did they only damage the rocks around us?"

He turned to Dirk. "Are you hurt?" he demanded. "Show me your back!"

Dirk hesitated, then, with a strange expression on his face, he turned so that Rye could see that the back of his shirt was whole and quite unmarked.

"There!" said Rye, fighting for calm. "You were between us and the bird, Dirk. Your back should be in tatters. And it is not!"

"No." Dirk looked over his shoulder and twisted his arm around to feel his back. He winced slightly. "It feels a little tender, that is all. As if it is bruised."

Rye shook his head in confusion. "Yet all around us the snails were torn from the rocks, and the rocks themselves were —"

He chanced to look down and saw with a small shock that the heaps of shells at his feet were moving. The snails were all calmly righting themselves and creeping slowly toward new resting places, slender tentacles waving in front of them.

"They were not damaged either," said Sonia, wrinkling her nose. "How strange! Their shells must be as strong as iron not to have been crushed by —"

She broke off with a gasp. Her head jerked up.

"The shell from the bag!" she exclaimed. "Rye! Its power must be —"

But Rye had had the same thought, at the same moment. He had spread out his hand. The snail shell he had taken from his pocket just moments before the monstrous bird attacked was jammed firmly over the tip of his little finger, covering the nail like a grotesque growth. Somehow, while he was clutching it, it had worked its way into place without his noticing.

"Armor," he breathed. He tugged experimentally at the shell, but it would not budge. He suspected it would remain part of him until it sensed he felt safe from attack. He knew he should be glad of it, but the sight of it made him feel sick.

"So!" Sonia cried, clapping her hands. She grinned fiercely up at Dirk's startled face. "You see? You did *nothing* to save us, Master Hero! As it happens, it was Rye's magic that saved *you*!"

Different expressions flitted across Dirk's face — anger, disbelief, confusion, embarrassment, and finally, acceptance.

"Well?" Sonia crowed. "What do you have to say for yourself now?"

Dirk took a breath. "There is nothing to say except that I am sorry," he said quietly. "I did not mean to claim thanks I did not deserve. I did not understand."

"Any more than we did!" Rye exclaimed, glancing angrily at Sonia.

But she was staring at Dirk, biting her lip, the spark of triumph slowly dying from her eyes. Dirk's frank readiness to admit he had been wrong had thrown her off balance. Suddenly, in one of the lightning changes of mood Rye had noticed in her before, she was ashamed of her gloating.

"You did deserve thanks," she said stiffly. "Nothing changes the fact that you risked your life trying to shield us. So I, too, apologize."

Now it was Dirk's turn to stare.

Sonia turned her head away, tearing off the dreadful Keep orphan's cap and shaking out her hair.

"So — which way should we go?" she asked, with a briskness that sounded completely false. "With cloud hiding the sun so completely, it is impossible to tell where north, south, east, and west might be."

Rye knew exactly what they should do, though the idea filled him with dread.

"There," he made himself say, pointing toward the place where the giant bird had disappeared into the clouds. "That bird is an evil thing. I think — I *know* — it is the Enemy's creature. If we wish to find him, and Sholto, we should follow it."

Sonia glanced at him, saw the certainty in his eyes, and instantly murmured agreement.

Dirk's brow creased. "But, Rye, how could you possibly *know* —?" he began, almost angrily. Then, no doubt remembering other strange things that his young brother had lately said and done, he changed his mind about what he had been going to say.

"I hope we are right in thinking Sholto chose the silver Door," he said instead. "I have seen no sign of him."

Rye looked up eagerly. "But we have!" he exclaimed. "We found his notebook — or what remained of it."

He felt in his pocket and pulled out the scraps of paper he had taken from the pyramid. He handed them to Dirk, who scanned them one after the other, his frown deepening as he read.

"I agree this is Sholto's writing," Dirk said after a moment. "But . . . I wish it were not."

"What do you mean?" Rye exclaimed. He snatched three of the paper scraps from Dirk's hand, and read the one on the top.

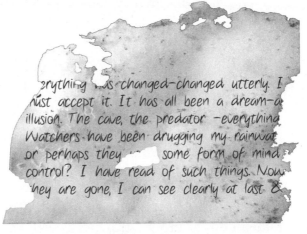

erything was changed-changed utterly. I
must accept it. It has all been a dream-a
illusion. The cave, the predator —everything
Watchers have been drugging my rainwa
or perhaps they   some form of mind
control? I have read of such things. Now
they are gone, I can see clearly at last &

"He was losing his mind," Dirk muttered.

"Not Sholto!" Rye said stoutly, though a heavy, sinking feeling was weighing him down. Quickly he glanced at the next fragment, very aware of Sonia crowding in to read over his shoulder.

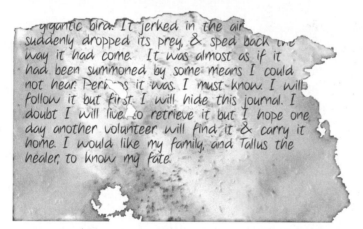

driving me mad. I cannot think. No food, v. little water. The snails will not open, even when roasted. No one comes. I cannot find the Door

Sonia made a small sound of distress. His mouth dry, Rye looked at the last fragment.

...gigantic bird. It jerked in the air suddenly dropped its prey, & sped back the way it had come. It was almost as if it had been summoned by some means I could not hear. Perhaps it was. I must know. I will follow it but first I will hide this journal. I doubt I will live to retrieve it but I hope one day another volunteer will find it & carry it home. I would like my family, and Tallus the healer, to know my fate.

FOLLOWING THE BIRD

In somber silence, Rye, Sonia, and Dirk built the pyramid up again. Then they set off across the snail-covered stones, trudging in the general direction the monster bird had taken.

At first, they had hoped that the red feather would help them glide above the rocks, but that idea had been quickly abandoned. The feather had lifted the three of them a little way off the ground, but with no wind to help them, and no trees they could use to pull themselves along, they had merely floated helplessly in one place, unable to move.

They could not use the horsehair ring either. Dirk insisted that speed would be dangerous.

"It is not just that the rocks are treacherous," he said as they began walking. "The earth in the bare patches, where the holes are, crumbles and caves in at a touch. And there are obstacles everywhere. The settlers use this wasteland as a rubbish dump, it seems. See here!"

With the toe of his boot, he nudged at a snail-covered object that Rye had taken to be a stone. As the object rolled, Rye made out a spout and a handle. He realized with astonishment that it was a kettle, just a little larger than the kettle his family had always used for heating water on the stove.

He shook his head in disbelief. The kettle was dented on one side, and there was a hole in its base, but what did that matter? It could be mended.

How could anyone throw away something so precious? The kettle at home in Southwall was a family heirloom, hundreds of years old, and polished and prized above anything else in the house.

"No doubt the snails eat the rest of the waste," Dirk said, kicking the kettle aside and moving on. "Only objects made of metal remain. When I was cleaning the skimmer hook I saw all manner of things — old tools, metal pipe, lengths of roofing iron . . ."

"But why would the people abandon such treasure?" Rye exclaimed.

Dirk laughed without humor. "In Weld, it is treasure, but outside the Wall, it is not. That was one of the things that most amazed me when I first realized it in Fleet. There is little metal in Dorne's earth, but metal is plentiful here all the same. Ships from other islands bring loads of it to Oltan, and they bring ready-made goods, too. Pots and pans, knives, nails, belt buckles, fish hooks, packets of pins and needles . . ."

He and Rye exchanged glances. Both were thinking of their mother's one precious steel sewing needle, handed down to her through the generations. It was worn fine as a hair, and kept for only the most important of mending tasks. Needles made of goat bone were used for everyday darning and patching.

The shared memory seemed to draw them closer, and apart from Sonia, child of the Keep. As if she sensed this, and resented it, Sonia looked at them sharply and spoke, shattering the mood.

"Well, if there is a lot of metal here, one mystery is solved, at least," she said. "We know that metal — especially iron — affects the magic of the powers in the bag. That is why the hood did not work as well as it should, even before Dirk came along with his hook. And that is very good news! It means that the snail shell will be even more powerful as protection once we are away from this place."

Rye nodded, frowning slightly. He had already worked that out and did not want to talk about it. For now, he did not want to think of the magic he carried, or of what the future might hold.

The warm memories of home had given him a moment's comfort, but they had brought Sholto vividly into his mind, too — Sholto as he had been, in the old days. Rye was haunted by the words he had read on the notebook fragments. It was terrible to think of his calm, clever brother crazed by hardship and loneliness, suffering delusions, fearing imaginary enemies, doubting his own sanity.

They trekked on, watching their feet and speaking very little. Giant insects soon came buzzing around them, and they were forced to walk awkwardly, with their hands linked, so that the snail shell on Rye's finger could protect them all. As Dirk had warned, countless obstacles lay strewn among the rocks, covered in snails and very hard to see. For all their care, Rye and Sonia stumbled often, and Dirk himself fell sprawling when his boot caught in a tangle of wire.

Strangely, this fall proved to be a stroke of good luck. As Dirk began clambering painfully to his feet, he suddenly stiffened and pointed to something ahead.

"There!" he gasped. "Rye, look there! I think . . . is that not another pyramid?"

It was. It was smaller than the one that had contained the remains of Sholto's notebook, and there was nothing inside it, but otherwise it was the same.

"It is a marker!" Dirk exclaimed, replacing the stones they had pulled from the top. "Sholto built markers so he could find his way back! What a miracle I saw it! By the Wall, Rye, we might have already passed a dozen of these without knowing it!"

"Hardly a dozen, if your brother did not spend more time building than walking," Sonia commented rather tartly.

But nothing could dampen the flame of hope that the second pyramid had raised in Rye and Dirk. It was not just that the marker proved that they were moving in the right direction. It was the knowledge that however disturbed Sholto had been he had not lost his natural caution or his instinct to plan, at least.

After this, they kept a sharp eye on the rocks ahead. Now and again they would be rewarded by the glimpse of another little pyramid, and they would vary their path to reach it.

At the sixth marker they stopped to eat, perching uncomfortably on a snail-covered rock only just big enough to seat them all. The food Sonia had stolen from the Keep kitchen tasted salty and faintly sour, as if the snails or the curling yellow mist had somehow tainted it. Rye had to force himself to take his share, and when they set off again, the meal seemed to lie like a heavy lump in his stomach.

They trudged on and on, following the pyramid trail. Slowly the light began to dim.

Rye noted the change, but he was too weary to feel more than a dull pang of fear. His whole body was aching. He longed to stop, to sit down and rest, but his pride would not allow him to do it. Sonia was ahead of him now, pulling him impatiently along. She seemed to have a new surge of energy. It was all he could do to keep up with her.

He saw Dirk glancing at the sky and knew what his brother was thinking. In an hour or two, the sun would set and the skimmers Sholto had seen would come out to hunt.

As if he had felt Rye's gaze, Dirk looked around. "We should stop and build a shelter for the night," he said.

Before Rye could answer, Sonia looked over her shoulder at them, shaking her head vehemently. "We cannot stop now!" she cried. "We are nearly there."

Dirk regarded her quizzically. Rye looked ahead. There was nothing to be seen but drifting veils of mist and endless snail-covered rocks glimmering very faintly in the fading light.

"We are nearly at the end of the wasteland," Sonia insisted. "Do you not feel it?"

"*Feel* it?" Dirk repeated blankly.

Sonia made an impatient sound. Her face was pale with exhaustion, but her eyes glowed with purpose. She tugged at Rye's hand.

"Come on!" she begged. "Just a little farther!"

"No, Sonia," Dirk said, calmly but very firmly. "Your longing to get out of this place is deceiving you. There is no sign whatever that the wasteland is coming to an end. We must stop and prepare for the night and the skimmers. It is too dangerous to do otherwise. We will have little enough time as it is."

"If Rye's shell could protect us from that giant bird it can surely protect us from skimmers!" Sonia argued, her voice rising. "We cannot stop so close to the end! We must go on! We must!"

Rye hesitated, torn, glancing from one to the other. Dirk was eyeing Sonia with concern. Clearly he thought she had taken leave of her senses, and certainly she looked wild enough, with her strained face and burning eyes.

Dirk's way was best, and safest. All Rye's common sense told him so, and all his instincts urged him to trust the brother he had looked up to all his life. But still he hesitated.

Sonia had been right before. She had been right in the Fell Zone.

He met Sonia's desperate gaze. He took a breath and suddenly noticed something.

"I think the air has become a little fresher," he said slowly. "Easier to breathe. As if —"

"Yes!" Sonia cried. "It is as I told you! The mist is ending! The snails are ending!"

Dirk shook his head. He, at least, had noticed no difference in the air.

But Rye had. He was almost sure of it. "Let us go on for a short while, Dirk," he coaxed. "Half an hour will not hurt."

"I will remind you of that when we are still building our shelter at sunset," Dirk said grimly. But as Sonia set off again, pulling Rye behind her, he followed.

As the minutes passed and the light continued to fade, Rye felt increasingly jittery. He was tormented by the fear that he had been wrong in taking Sonia's side. And he had begun to feel he was being watched.

I am just very tired, he told himself as, for the fifth or sixth time, he jerked his head up and saw nothing to fear. *This place is affecting me. I am imagining things, as Sholto did.*

But the feeling would not leave him. His vision blurred as he peered into the misty distance. Then his mouth went dry. He could swear that the land ahead had begun to quiver!

He rubbed his eyes, but it made no difference. It was only when he looked down at the rocks beneath his feet that he realized what was happening.

Slender tentacles were emerging from all the patterned shells. The tentacles were waving like blades of grass stirred by a breeze, making the rocks appear to tremble.

"The snails are waking," he murmured.

"They sense the day is ending," Dirk said, his voice full of meaning. "No doubt they feed in the coolness of the night."

"All the more reason why we should not be here when the sun goes down," Sonia snapped. "I do not like the idea of sleeping in a shelter crawling with snails that will eat anything and are impossible to kill!"

"If Rye's shell can protect us from skimmers, it can protect us from a few snails!" Dirk snapped back.

"A *few!*" Sonia jeered, and hurried on.

As Rye stumbled after her, he could not stop thinking about what she had said. The thought of being overwhelmed by snails in their millions made his stomach heave. It was almost worse than the idea of skimmers. At least that death would be quick.

He smiled grimly. Snails or skimmers — what a choice!

"There!"

Sonia's triumphant cry rang out, startlingly loud. Rye looked up quickly.

A new pyramid lay ahead. It was taller than the last few they had seen. Only a few snails dotted its surface, and none of them were moving. Beside the pyramid, a post that might once have supported a sign leaned drunkenly to one side. And beyond it, there was a dusty plain, bare and unwelcoming but blessedly free of rocks and yellow mist.

The companions scrambled over the last of the treacherous stones and slid with relief onto clear ground. The pyramid rose before them, dark against the treeless landscape. Only then did they see that the tilting post beside it marked the beginning of a deeply worn pebbled track that stretched away to the dim horizon.

"The end!" Sonia crowed, clapping her hands. "We have reached the end!"

A figure unfolded itself from behind the pyramid. It was a man, extremely tall, and so thin that he might have been a skeleton. He was wearing nothing but a faded piece of cloth roughly tied around his waist and several strings of oddly shaped beads. His hair stood up in white spikes all over his head like the crest of a stalker bird.

The companions yelled in shock. Dirk's skimmer hook was in his hand in an instant, and Rye snatched the bell tree stick from his belt, forgetting all about the armor shell.

The stranger laughed. His mouth was so enormously wide that it looked as if his face had split in half. Rye saw in horror that he had no teeth.

"The end!" the skeleton man shrieked. "Yes, oh, yes indeed, my lords an' lady! See here!"

He bent from the waist like a folding ruler. When he straightened, he was holding up a rusty metal sign that had no doubt fallen from the crooked post.

BONES

The skeleton man watched avidly as Rye, Sonia, and Dirk read the sign. "Bones sees!" he cackled. "Bones sees your eyes a-reading along! You know your words all right, lords an' lady! See this one?" With a long yellow fingernail, he stabbed at the word "death."

"Stay where you are," Dirk murmured to Rye and Sonia, his lips barely moving. He stepped forward, tightening his grip on the skimmer hook.

"That's 'death' that is," the skeleton man said, nodding madly. "That's one Bones knows." He jabbed at the third word on the sign. "An' 'Saltings,' that's another."

"Indeed," Dirk agreed politely. "And what of this?" Without taking his eyes off the stranger, he pointed to the strange symbol that followed the warning message.

Bones blinked rapidly. His hand crept up to the beads hanging around his neck, and he began to finger them one by one, muttering under his breath. With a thrill of disgust, Rye realized for the first time that they were not beads at all, but human teeth.

"Well?" Dirk asked roughly, tapping the symbol.

Bones cringed. "Is the mark," he mumbled, his ridged yellow nails clicking feverishly on his repulsive necklace. "*His* mark. The Master."

The last words were no more than a hoarse whisper. Rye's own spine tingled in response to the man's terror. He felt Sonia grip his arm, but did not turn to look at her. He could not tear his eyes away from the symbol on the sign.

It was just a hand enclosed in a circle. There was a fuzzy white spot in the center of the hand's palm, as if a light was burning there. Surely there was nothing so terrible in that. Yet as he stared at it, Rye felt dread gathering like a cold cloud around his heart.

"The Master," Dirk repeated slowly. "Your master rules this side of Dorne, does he?"

Bones stared, his mouth hanging open. "Bones don't know sides," he said at last. "Bones only knows the Scour, an' the Saltings."

"What — where — is the Scour?" Dirk snapped.

Bones waved his arm helplessly at the flat, bare land. "All here, till where the Saltings starts."

"And it is death to enter the Saltings, is it?"

Again Bones nodded. And then, weirdly, though his eyes remained fearful, his lips twisted into a crooked smile. He looked over his shoulder as if to make absolutely sure that no one else was listening. Then he leaned forward.

"For most it is," he whispered. "But not for Bones. Bones be too much for the Master that way. An' not for you, lords an' lady — no, no, no! You be too much for the Master as well, you three."

A look of cunning appeared on his face. He tapped the side of his nose.

"Bones knows. Bones sees it with his own two eyes! Hand in hand you comes, treading the Saltings like the wizard kings in the ol' tales. You sees the castles of stones, an' you follow, follow. An' the whiners, big as they are, and hungry for your blood, they don't dare come near."

"You were watching us!" Impulsively Rye moved forward, ignoring Dirk's angry hiss of warning. "I felt you, but I could not see you!"

The thin man tittered. "No one sees Bones in the Saltings. Bones squirms on his belly in the Saltings, flat as a twisty snake. You don't see Bones. But Bones sees you!"

His cackling broke off in a squeak of fright as Dirk lunged for him, reaching for his throat. With a cry, Rye threw himself between them, and Dirk staggered back with a grunt of anger and surprise as the armor shell repelled him.

"Let him be, Dirk!" Rye yelled. "He is harmless."

"Harmless?" Dirk spat. "He was spying on us! By the Wall, he was taunting us with it! This is no time for squeamishness, Rye. Stand aside and leave this to me!"

But Rye shook his head. He could feel the old man's confusion as well as his fear. And with a colder part of his mind, he knew that Bones would tell them far more if they were kind to him than if they threatened him.

He turned to Bones, who was cringing against the pyramid, frantically clicking his horrible beads.

"I am sorry, Bones," he said gently. "My brother was mistaken. He thought you were threatening us."

"Bones is no spy," the old man croaked. "The Master has spies — many an' many! But Bones is not one of them. Bones is . . . only Bones."

"We understand that now," Rye said, still in that same gentle voice. "You have no more to fear from us."

Bones wet his lips and at last nodded warily. Rye beckoned urgently to Dirk and Sonia. Dirk, his face thunderous, took no notice, but Sonia moved cautiously forward.

"We are glad to meet you, sir," she murmured, dropping one of her surprisingly graceful curtseys.

The curtsey looked as odd as ever to Rye. No doubt it was perfectly proper in the Keep of Weld, but it contrasted very strangely with Sonia's grubby orphan clothes.

Bones, however, was clearly impressed. His face full of awe, he abruptly folded his angular body into a bow so deep that his nose nearly touched his knees.

"A honor," he mumbled, straightening with a great rattling of beads and cracking of joints. "A honor, great lady!"

"Bones," Rye said carefully, "is there somewhere nearby where we could talk in safety?"

Bones's mouth stretched into that impossibly wide toothless grin. "'Course!" he crowed. "Den's not far up along. Wait! Wait!"

He jumped off the track and loped away to the left, the tooth necklaces bouncing and clicking on his chest. Reaching a low hump in the ground, he bent and began to scrabble in the earth, throwing dust aside by the handful.

Rye glanced at Dirk, who was clearly still very angry. "I am sorry, Dirk," he said in a low voice. "But you were wrong. Bones is no danger to us, and he can help us — I know he can."

"And I know that you are listening to your heart instead of your head," Dirk growled. "You are not in Weld now, Rye! You are not even in the part of Dorne we know. Olt's sorcerer brother rules here, and by the sound of it, he is worse than Olt himself. Bones is terrified of him, and ten to one will betray us!"

"What is he doing?" Sonia whispered, jerking her head at the old man, who was now almost hidden in the cloud of dust he had raised.

"Digging up something he has buried, by the looks of it," said Dirk in disgust. "By the Wall, the sun will be setting soon. How long do we have to wait?"

But in fact Bones had not buried his treasure, it seemed. He had just disguised it under a thin layer of dirt so it would be safe from prying eyes. The hump in the ground was quickly revealed to be a large object draped in a cloth made of many odd pieces of fabric sewn together. Bones glanced at the companions and, having made sure that they were watching, triumphantly whipped away the cloth, showering himself with dust.

The thing beneath the cloth was a large sled with two long shafts at one end. It looked a little like one of the sleds that Weld Wall workers used to move loads of newly made bricks across the slick, wet mud of the trench. It was heaped high with what looked like pieces of bleached wood.

Bones draped the cloth around his shoulders like a cloak and knotted two of its corners under his chin. Then he backed into the space between the sled's shafts. Gripping one shaft in each enormous hand, he came lolloping back, the sled bumping behind him.

As the sled slid down onto the pebbles of the track, Rye caught his breath. The entire vehicle was made of bones lashed together with leather thongs and rusty wire. Most were too large to be goat bones and too small to have belonged to a horse. Rye could not imagine what animal they had come from. And the load was not wood, but a mass of even larger bones — the biggest Rye had ever seen. Right in the center of the sled, carefully wedged in so it would not be damaged, was a vast animal skull from which jutted a wickedly sharp yellow-white horn.

"By the Wall — a cursed bloodhog!" Dirk muttered, unconsciously rubbing the healed wound on his side.

Sonia wrinkled her nose in disgusted horror. No doubt, Rye thought in grim amusement, animal skeletons were not everyday sights in the polite world of the Keep. They had become all too familiar in the rest of Weld since the skimmer invasions began.

"Out of the sky he come!" Bones grinned, plainly delighted by their reactions. "A wonder, it were! Sky serpent bird, he lets ol' bloodhog go, right up high, an' down ol' bloodhog come, bang into the Saltings! Never did Bones see such a thing in all his born days!"

With a stab of excitement, Rye remembered a very similar story told on one of the scraps of Sholto's notebook. Sholto, too, had seen a gigantic bird suddenly drop its prey and fly away.

Had Sholto and Bones both witnessed the same event? Surely they had, if Bones thought it such a wonder. And that meant that Bones and Sholto had been in this area on the same day. They might even have met, as Sholto left the Saltings!

Rye longed to question the old man about it but decided it was better to wait until they were on their way. The light was fading fast now, and Dirk was glancing uneasily at the cloudy sky.

Bones seemed quite unconcerned by the approach of night. He was nodding happily.

"Big ol' bloodhog!" he crowed. "He be treasure for Bones an' the Den when he all picked clean, Bones says to hisself when he sees him first. An' today he be finished, shiny white, so Bones loads him an' brings him out. An' while he's a-doing that, Bones sees you! So Bones hides sled while he waits. An' out you comes from the Saltings, sure enough! An' now here we all is, good as gold!"

He turned his gummy grin on Sonia and gestured proudly at the sled. "Climb on, lady!" he said. "You be riding in fine style, as is fitting."

"Oh no!" Sonia exclaimed, backing away from the bloodhog skull in horror.

"Sonia means that she would far rather walk with you, Bones," Rye put in quickly, seeing the old man's face fall. "But she thanks you kindly for your offer."

He glared at Sonia until she forced a feeble smile and nodded.

Bones looked at her admiringly. "A true an' gracious lady, you," he said. "A fine lady, like in the olden tales. Walk with Bones, then, and we'll go up along like friends together."

"Is this Den place far from here?" Dirk demanded, glancing yet again at the sky.

"A step or two," grinned Bones. "But don't you mind about it — sky's a-darkening now, an' ol' sky serpents, they hunt in the light."

Rye wet his lips. "But surely sky serpents are not the only dangers," he said. "Are there no other flying creatures to fear by night?"

"No, no!" Bones said in obvious surprise. "Night's safe . . . 'cept for bloodhogs, an' they be few in the Scour these days. Sky serpents has got most of 'em."

He waited courteously until Sonia and Rye had moved to his right hand side, and Dirk, frowning in puzzlement, had taken the place on his left. Then he seized the shafts of his sled and set off along the pebbly track at a great pace, with his companions hurrying along beside him.

"Bones," Rye began, raising his voice to compete with the dull roar of the sled's runners rasping over the pebbles of the track, "how well do you remember the day when the bloodhog fell into the Saltings? I know it must have been a long time ago, but —"

Bones cackled. "A sad ol' change it'll be when Bones don't bemember that far back! Why, only three days past, it were, counting this one just ended!"

Swallowing a groan of disappointment, Rye tried to return the old man's grin. Sholto had left Weld over a year ago. He could not have been in the Saltings all that time. How could he have survived?

Clearly, Dirk thought Bones was lying or simply had no idea of time.

"Three days ago? That would mean the snails stripped a bloodhog to bare bones in *two nights*," he scoffed, jerking his head at the sled's rattling cargo.

Bones nodded violently. "Yes, indeed, lords an' lady. A man, now — a man lays down in the dark, anytime, an' by dawning, he's a-picked clean, ready for Bones to collect. But ol' bloodhog, he took two full nights! That's how big he were."

Rye's stomach turned over. He glanced across the sled at Dirk. Dirk stared back, his eyes dark with horror.

"So the Saltings is clearly no place to spend the night," Sonia muttered.

Rye jerked his head around to look at her. Sonia's face showed nothing but pleasure at having been proved right. Either she had not heard what Bones had said about collecting human bones, or she had not thought about what it might mean.

Rye turned his eyes to the front again, forcing himself not to look at the smooth white bones of the sled — the bones that were too big for a goat, and too small for a horse, but were just right for a human being.

THE MOUNDS

*F*orget the sled, Rye told himself firmly. *Forget what Bones collects in the Saltings. The important thing is that he visits the place often — maybe every day! He still might have seen Sholto. Concentrate on that — think only of that. And ask Bones about it, while you have the chance.*

"Bones, about the pyramids — the castles of stones — in the Saltings," he managed to say. "Did you see the man who made them? Did you speak to him?"

Bones nodded, then shook his head. Sweat had already begun dripping down his hollow cheeks, making long, clean lines in the film of dust.

"Bones sees sure enough, but that day, Bones has better business than talking to wanderers doomed to die. That day, Bones be squirming in the Saltings like a twisty snake, to find where bloodhog corpus lies so to take the skin afore night come. Bones sees wanderer piling stone on stone and he thinks, by tomorrow's dawning he'll be a skelington, that fellow, ripe for picking. An' maybe ol' bloodhog, too! But ol' bloodhog, he took longer."

Rye's breath caught in his throat, and his stomach twisted into a hard, painful knot. He could feel Dirk's eyes burning into him but refused to look around.

Was it possible? Was it possible that, after all, Sholto had left the Saltings only three days ago? Perhaps. Perhaps he had set up camp in a place of safety — some part of the wasteland Rye, Dirk, and Sonia had not seen.

"You were wrong, though, Bones," Rye said, fighting to keep his voice even. "That man did *not* die in the Saltings, did he? He reached the end, as we did. He made that pile of stones back there, where we met you."

"So he do!" Bones nodded enthusiastically, pop-eyed with remembered surprise. "Well, there's another wonder, Bones says to hisself, when he sees that castle rearing up by the Master's sign next dawning. Ho, wonders be coming thick an' fast these days, Bones says to hisself. Omens they be, for certain sure, of a even greater wonder to come. An' so Bones tells them all, at the Den, an' now they'll find out ol' Bones spoke true. 'Cos here you be, lords an' lady! Here you be, good as gold!"

"Is that why you waited to talk to us?" gasped Rye, his chest aching with the effort of talking and running at the same time. "Because you thought —"

"That's it!" The old man glanced from side to side, greedily drinking in the sight of his companions. "Bones sees you and straightaway Bones knows magic abides with you. Bones smells it!"

He ducked his head at Sonia and showed his gums. Her face froze.

"Like flowers, it is," the old man whispered. "Like new grass growing. Like clear water bubbling. Like the air at dawning afore . . ."

For a moment, his watery eyes stared blankly, as if they were seeing something other than the pebbled track, the bleak horizon. Then he blinked, and his face brightened as he looked quickly from side to side again.

"You be a wonder, you three," he said, nodding as he raced along, the sled rattling and roaring behind him. "Hand in hand through the Saltings you comes. An' Bones says to hisself, there'll be nothing for you out of this, ol' fellow! The hungry shells won't get those three an' turn them to skelingtons in the dark, no fear! They'll come to the end on their own legs, like the wizards of old. And so you do, lords an' lady, so you do!"

Abruptly he swerved off the track to the left and began dragging the clattering sled over rougher ground where a few tufts of grass struggled for life.

Ahead, a cluster of low dirt mounds rose against the dull red sky.

"Ho!" Bones bawled at the top of his voice. "Come see! Bones has got magic ones here! Magic lords an' lady to save us all! Come see, me hearties! Come see!"

Puffs of dust began to erupt from the blunt tips of the mounds. The puffs became clouds, and powdery earth began to trickle downward. In moments, every mound had sprouted a tousled head, and dozens of startled eyes were peering at the newcomers.

"Come see!" Bones cried, beckoning madly.

People began crawling out of the mounds. The sight was eerie and very disturbing. It was like watching the dead rising from their graves.

The mound people wore a bizarre assortment of rags in many different styles, and under the dust it was clear that their hair and skin were of many different shades. But all of them looked past middle age, all were as wretchedly thin as Bones, and, most startling of all, their hands and wrists were stained bright red, as if they had been dipped in blood.

Cursing under his breath, Dirk stepped quickly over the sled shafts to join Rye and Sonia.

"What has happened to their hands?" Sonia whispered, staring at the walking skeletons.

"Jell-stained, by the look of it," Dirk said. He glanced at her, saw that she had no idea what he was talking about, and shook his head.

"I daresay you have never dug in the earth in your life, Sonia," he said, with a trace of scorn. "If you had, you would know that every now and then you break into a seam of jell. Jell is bright red, soft as butter, and stains whatever it touches. It is a great nuisance in the Wall trench. Even a trace of it spoils a brick — stops the mud from drying. It has to be cleared away very carefully, using thick gloves to protect the skin."

"Indeed," Sonia replied with icy politeness. "Well, thank you for the lecture — though perhaps you could have saved the boring details for another time, when we are not about to be overwhelmed by —"

"Hush," Rye hissed. "Be still, and for Weld's sake, look confident! Bones has told these people we are wizards, so wizards we must be."

And if they want magic, we will show them some, he thought. He touched the armor shell to make sure it was still fixed securely on his little finger. He took Sonia's arm, and, understanding, she took Dirk's.

The moving people were closer now. Rye could see their starved faces, their hollow, staring eyes.

At the head of a crowd was a haggard woman. Her long gray-streaked black hair had fallen out in patches, and what was left hung in greasy tails around her face. A knife of sharpened bone hung from a cord at her waist. As she walked, she muttered to the two gaunt men on either side of her, barely moving her lips. The men nodded slightly. Rye saw that they, too, carried knives in their belts.

"I do not like the look of that trio," Dirk growled.

"Whatever happens, do not move," Rye muttered back. "Trust the shell. We must convince them —"

"What is this, Bones?" demanded a limping man who was leaning on a stick and whose beaky nose and sunken eyes were almost completely hidden by his matted hair and beard. "You know better than to bring strangers here."

"Come see, Cap!" shouted Bones. Springing into the crowd, he seized the speaker's arm and bustled him forward. As the man came fully into view, Rye saw with a shock that he limped because his right leg had been replaced below the knee with a peg of bone.

"Out of the Saltings they come, Cap, good as gold!" chattered Bones, gesturing grandly at Rye, Dirk, and Sonia as if he was presenting royalty. "They be too much for the Master, these three!"

The crowd murmured, eyeing the visitors suspiciously. The haggard woman spat contemptuously in the dust.

"Watch your tongue, Bones!" the one-legged man warned.

Bones laughed uproariously. "Bones says what he likes now, Cap!" he caroled. "Us be all safe now, me hearty! Magic ones be with us now!"

"They're spies, you dunderhead!" the haggard woman said in a low, rasping voice. "More of the Master's spies! *Now*!"

As she shouted the last word, she and the two men flanking her snatched their knives from their belts and threw themselves at Rye, Dirk, and Sonia.

The attack was so sudden, and so violent, that even though Rye had been half expecting it, he found it impossible not to flinch. But his terror lasted only a split second. One moment, his ears were ringing with

Cap's angry shout and Bones's shrieks of protest, and all he could see were bared teeth, red-stained hands, and the wicked points of knives. The next moment, the three attackers had bounced backward and were sprawling in the dust at his feet.

Cries of fear and amazement rose from the crowd. Many people fell to their knees, crossing their fingers and their wrists. Bones howled with delight.

"Bones told you!" he yelled, capering around the three on the ground, his dusty cloak flapping like the wings of some tall, bony bird. "Magic ones! Come out of the Saltings to save us, as was foretold!"

"Shut your mouth, you crazy old fool!" the woman snarled. Sullenly she clambered to her feet, dusting her hands on her filthy skirt, which seemed to have been made from the remnants of many other garments roughly cobbled together. The two men stood up, too, glowering and rubbing their heads.

"Sorcerers!" one of them said bitterly. "You've brought death to us all, Bones — death, or worse. They're servants of the Master!"

"We are no one's servants!" cried Sonia, her eyes blazing in fury, her face still pale with the shock of the attack. "How dare you say so? Your tyrant master is as much our enemy as he is yours!"

The kneeling people cowered, darting terrified looks at the sky. Bones whimpered, rattling his beads in agitation.

"There!" shrieked the haggard woman. "She's

trying to trick us into betraying ourselves! Only see the magic crackling in her hair and sparking from her witch's eyes!"

"You have nothing to fear from us, I swear it," Rye said, glancing angrily at Sonia, who tossed her head and turned away. "We mean you no harm!"

"If we did, we would have done far more than simply defend ourselves when we were attacked, I assure you," Dirk added quietly, raising the skimmer hook.

In the dead silence that followed, the one-legged man called Cap limped forward, leaning heavily on his stick. He pushed aside his straggly hair and peered first at Dirk, then at Sonia and Rye. His eyes were gray and very shrewd.

"You see it, Cap?" Bones begged. "You see how it was right to bring them up along? You feel the wonder of them?"

"Yes indeed," Cap said slowly, his eyes still fixed on the visitors. "You can leave them in my care now, Bones. Take the sled over to the Den, there's a good fellow. Four-Eyes will be by very soon and we don't want to miss him, do we? Not tonight."

Bones hesitated, glancing uncertainly from Rye, Sonia, and Dirk to his loaded sled as if he could not decide which he valued more.

"Go, Bones," his leader coaxed. "You'll move more quickly alone. If Four-Eyes comes, let him look, but on no account agree to a trade. I'll be with you as soon as I can."

Bones gave a shuddering sigh and nodded. He bowed to Rye, Dirk, and Sonia and backed between the shafts of the sled. As he turned the vehicle around, the watching people gained a clear view of the great pile of bones and the mighty skull of the bloodhog for the first time. The sight seemed to drive everything else from their minds. They all jumped up, exclaiming in excitement.

Bones's hollow chest swelled. His face split into a gummy grin. "Told you!" he bellowed over his shoulder. "Told you ol' bloodhog were a wonder! Wait till Four-Eyes sees him! Ho, we'll feast tonight, me hearties!"

The sled rattling behind him, he loped back the way he had come, quickly disappearing into the gathering shadows.

"May a sky serpent take the old loon!" the haggard woman muttered.

"Take care what you wish for, Needle," Cap replied mildly. "Who else would dare enter the Saltings and bring out the bones that keep us all alive? You?"

Needle scowled and turned away.

"Finish here while I deal with our guests," Cap called to the gaping, whispering crowd. "Floss, will you —?"

"Oh yes, I'll bring your pickings along, Cap, for what they're worth," grinned an old woman whose skin was so webbed with fine lines that it looked like well-used leather. "It's painful enough watching you climb down the hole once a day, without watching you do it twice."

"So kind," the man replied with a smile and a mocking bow.

The exchange broke the tension. A few people laughed. Needle and her two henchmen scrambled up a large mound and crawled into the hole at the top one by one. Then Floss and the others disappeared into their own mounds, and soon only Rye, Sonia, Dirk, and Cap remained above ground.

In the silence that followed, the companions became aware of an ominous growling, panting sound in the distance. Rye's skin prickled. He felt Sonia grip his arm more tightly.

"What is that?" Dirk asked sharply.

"Nothing that concerns you," snapped Cap, whose smile had vanished the moment they were alone. "Come with me."

FOUR-EYES

Cap turned away from the mounds and began limping along the trail left by the runners of the sled. "Take care to tread where I tread," he called back over his shoulder. "The ground's not safe."

Rye, Sonia, and Dirk followed cautiously, hands linked. By now, it was almost completely dark. The panting sound was growing louder by the moment, but Cap did not speak again. Only when they had reached the track and scrambled down onto its pebbled surface did he turn to face them.

The marks of Bones's sled continued across the track and disappeared into the darkness on the other side, but clearly Cap did not plan to take his guests any farther. He had no intention of offering them shelter for the night.

Rye found himself feeling quite shocked. Even before the skimmer attacks began, no citizen of Weld would have dreamed of turning a traveler away at nightfall.

You are not in Weld now, Rye.

Indeed, Rye thought grimly.

"This will lead you out of the Scour," Cap was saying rapidly to Dirk, pointing along the track. "Don't stray from it or you'll come to grief — the land on either side is studded with old jell pits. Only those who know what they're doing can navigate it. Trust no one. There are spies everywhere."

He glanced at Rye and Sonia, then looked quickly back at Dirk, frowning with distaste. "And for pity's sake, make those two cover their hair," he added. "Nothing is more likely to betray you."

Rye found his fisherman's cap and pulled it on. Sonia looked mutinous, then seemed to decide that the advice was good even if she resented the way it had been given. Silently she twisted her hair into a knot and snuffed out its brilliance with the ugly cloth helmet of the Keep orphan.

"The track runs past the Diggings," Cap was telling Dirk. "If you manage to pass them in safety, which I doubt, it will take you on to where you want to go."

"And how do you know where we wish to go?" Dirk asked coolly.

Cap snorted. "Do you take me for a fool? Even if I hadn't heard your copper-head friend shout her feelings to the skies, there's only one reason for people like you to have risked your lives trekking over the Saltings. You've come from across the sea to spy on the Master. Perhaps you even have orders to destroy him."

Before Rye, Dirk, or Sonia could speak, he held up his hands.

"Tell me nothing! The less I know of you, the better. Whatever you're planning, whatever powers you have, you've no hope of defeating the Master. His sorcery is too powerful. One way or another, your mission will end in your deaths. But I daresay there's no hope of persuading you of that, so I won't waste my breath trying."

He looked across the track as the panting noise suddenly stopped and a low hissing floated from the gloom.

"Go now!" he ordered. "I've given you all the help I can."

"You do not have to live like this any longer, Cap," Dirk burst out impulsively, gripping the other man's shoulder. "You can get your people away. The other side of Dorne is safe now. We —"

"Stop!" Cap snarled, tearing himself free. "Keep your idiot thoughts to yourself, I tell you! Do you think we'd be here if there were any hope of escape? We're watched continually. Our borders are sealed. The Saltings is death. We're prisoners as surely as if we were behind iron bars, and we remain alive only because we're no threat to the Master and too old or crippled to be put to work in the Diggings."

He glared at the companions through the tangles of his matted hair. "If you truly mean us no harm, you'll go, and go quickly. In general, we're left alone, but if you're seen here, you'll attract attention we can well do without. Do you understand?"

Dirk nodded, clearly moved by the man's plain speaking. Hoisting his skimmer hook more firmly onto his shoulder, he turned toward the dark horizon, trying to pull Rye and Sonia with him.

But Rye stood his ground. Cap's voice had been steady but his nerves were strung as tightly as a trip wire — Rye could feel it. The man certainly *did* want to be rid of his unwelcome guests before they were seen. But this was not the only reason he was hurrying them away.

He was hiding something, and he wanted Dirk, Rye, and Sonia to leave before they found it out. It was something to do with whatever was hissing in the darkness on the other side of the track. And it involved Sholto, too. Rye had never been so certain of anything in his life.

A terrible fear gripped his heart. "One thing, before we go," he said abruptly. "We are searching for one of our own who is missing — a thin, dark-haired man of about your height. Have you seen him?"

Cap ducked his shaggy head so they could not

see his face. "I've seen no one of that description," he said. "Sorry."

A weird, yodeling cry floated from the gloom beyond the track. Cap's head jerked up. "I must go," he said. "Travel safely."

Without another word, he swung himself off the track and began hobbling rapidly toward the sound.

"He is lying," Rye muttered. "Or at least he is not telling the whole truth."

"You are right," Sonia agreed. "He chose his words very carefully. Perhaps he did not see Sholto with his own eyes, but he knows something."

"Rubbish!" Dirk snapped. "You are imagining things, the two of you. The man has helped us as much as he can. We should do as he asks, and leave him alone. By the Wall, is his life not hard enough, with that motley, quarrelling crew to lead and protect? The best thing we can do for him is to get away before that lunatic Bones fastens upon us again."

He tugged Rye's arm but Rye still resisted, shaking his head, and Sonia made no move to walk on either.

"This is madness!" Dirk hissed. "Rye, do as I tell you! Who is the leader here?"

"No one!" Sonia flashed back. "You may be older, Dirk of Southwall, and a great hero in Weld, but as you are so fond of telling us, we are not in Weld now! As far as I am concerned, we are all equal in this. If Rye senses there is a secret to be uncovered and I agree with him, then that is the end of it. Believe your precious Cap and go on alone if you will!"

Dirk's face darkened and Rye felt a stab of panic.

"No!" he exclaimed. "We must stay together." He pulled the hood of concealment over his head. "There! Now if we link arms we will not be seen."

"The skimmer hook is metal," Sonia warned. "It will still be visible."

"Just as a shadow," Rye said quickly, as Dirk scowled. "The darkness should cover it."

He turned to his brother. "Dirk, all I ask is that we listen a while. If we hear nothing of Sholto, we can leave as quietly as we came. Cap need never know we followed him."

Dirk hesitated, then sighed heavily and nodded.

They set off after Cap, following the sled tracks and keeping well back. It was dark but not so dark that they could not see the limping figure ahead. At first, the man kept looking over his shoulder but at last seemed satisfied that he was not being followed. He put his head down and hurried on, very quickly considering his handicap.

"For a half-starved man with only one leg, he manages very well," Sonia whispered.

"They all manage very well," said Rye, thinking of Bones, Needle, and the old woman Cap had called Floss. "If they are indeed some of the exiles from Oltan, they have been seven years in this barren wilderness!

It is amazing that they have survived, let alone that they are so strong."

"The weaker ones among them died early on, no doubt," Dirk said soberly. "Only the strong remain."

His mouth tightened. "It is . . . a terrible thing. They came here to escape Olt, following a leader they trusted, only to find themselves trapped in a situation that is even worse than the one they fled. And the people they left behind have no idea!"

"I would not have trusted any brother of Olt's," Sonia said.

Dirk shot her a sour look. "You do not know what you might have done if you were desperate."

Sonia shook her head stubbornly.

Ahead, a small light was showing, and shadows were dancing on the ground. The weird cry came again. Cap gave a hoarse answering shout and increased his speed.

As the companions hurried after him, they realized that the yodeling sound had come from Bones — Bones, who was dancing about in front of his sled, holding a flaming torch high, his skull-like face ghastly in the flickering light.

He was facing a monstrous, hissing shape that loomed above him in a cloud of steam.

Rye's heart seemed to stop. For a split second, he thought that the old man was protecting his treasure from some huge, ferocious beast. Then he realized that the hissing object was in fact some sort of gigantic vehicle.

The thing had no shafts, and no goats or horses to draw it. It was made of many odd sheets of metal bolted together, and was very strangely shaped — rather like a monstrous, armored turtle with a high square shell. In place of wheels, it had vast metal rollers. Steam billowed from a chimney at its nose, and a rusty tank bulged at its rear. On its battered side was a vividly colored sign that had clearly been painted in haste by an untrained hand.

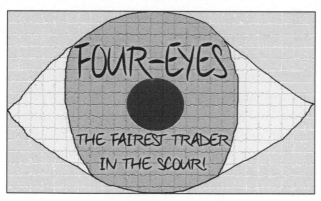

"Ho, Cap!" Bones shrieked, leaping and waving as he sighted the one-legged man. "Four-Eyes says five shivs of tarny root, half a shiv of sea biscuit, an' a bunch of travel weed for ol' bloodhog skull!"

"Not near enough," Cap shouted back.

"Bones knows it!" cried the capering man. "Bones tells him! You cheated Bones last time, Four-Eyes, Bones tells him — Cap says you did!"

"Keep your voice down!" Cap ordered, glancing nervously over his shoulder. "Leave this to me."

"There!" bawled Bones, shaking his fist at the hissing monstrosity. "That be telling you, Four-Eyes! You won't be cheating Cap — oh no!"

A rich laugh rolled from the steam.

"Now, Bones, my old friend!" boomed a deep voice. "I wish I had something truly worthy to trade for your treasure, but I can't give what I don't have, can I? My supplies are very low just now. And what's all this talk of cheating? Why, I'm the fairest trader in all the Scour. My new sign tells you so! As you would know if you could read it."

"You can't read it neither, Four-Eyes!" Bones bawled. "An' if it tells what you says it tells, it's a liar!"

"Now, take care what you say, my friend," the voice said, a hard edge entering the rich tones. "You are hurting my feelings. 'Liar' is a strong word — very strong. And so is 'cheat,' come to that. Why, it almost makes me want to leave you alone entirely! And how would you good people get along, I ask you, without the food I bring?"

"Ha!" cried Bones. "Little you knows, Four-Eyes! Us has magic ones to aid us now — wizards out of the Saltings! Food us'll have in plenty, in days to come, an' golden bowls to eat it out of, too!"

Rye felt himself grow hot. He heard Sonia groan softly beside him, and Dirk grunt in disgust.

"Bones!" thundered Cap. "Be still!"

But Bones was beyond listening to orders. He was shaking his fist at the vehicle, fairly dancing with rage. And what he said next chilled Rye's blood.

"Cap says stranger's clothes an' boots an' bag of treasures was worth three times over what you give for them, Four-Eyes! You catched Bones on the track alone an' you bedazzled him with your smoothy talk an' your smiling ways!"

"Dearie me!" sighed the voice from the steam. "How could Cap say such a thing? As I remember, it was a *very* fair trade."

"Well, it weren't!" Bones bawled. "Six strips of salty goat an' half a shiv of tarny root you give for the lot! Cap says Bones'd have done better to keep all stranger's riches safe for the Den! Then us could've used them for the good of all — same as next day us used his bones!"

THE DEN

irk's arm tensed till it felt like rock beneath
Rye's hand. Rye tightened his grip, warning
Dirk to keep silent. His own mind was reeling
with what he had heard, but he knew it was vital that
Cap, Bones, and the trader did not suspect that they
were being overheard. The whole story had not yet
been told.

"Wait!" he breathed in Dirk's ear.

Dirk glanced at him furiously, showing the
whites of his eyes. Rye understood. Dirk was wild with
anger because Cap had lied to him. He was mad
with grief at the thought that clever, funny, determined
Sholto might be dead, his possessions traded for scraps
of food, and his bones used to repair Bones's sled. He
wanted to spring out of hiding, confront Cap and
Bones, force them to admit what had been done —
what Needle and her two henchmen had done, perhaps,

with their deadly knives and their fear of the Master's spies.

Rye felt the same. But . . .

He met Sonia's serious green eyes. She nodded and put a finger to her lips.

"Be still, Dirk!" he hissed. "Be still and listen!"

With relief, he felt Dirk's arm relax slightly and heard his brother breathe out.

Cap had reached Bones. He was speaking to the frenzied man in a low voice, trying to calm him. He was shooting warning looks into the steam, too, as if advising Four-Eyes the trader to say no more.

Rye, Sonia, and Dirk crept closer. They saw that the sled had been pulled up beside a flat bridge that was a simple raft of bones lashed together with strings of leather. The bridge spanned a wide, deep trench, the base of which was studded with spears of sharpened bone, their shafts buried, their wicked points aiming at the sky.

On the other side of the trench was a long, low hut. Beside the hut, there was the gleam of water, the first the companions had seen in this barren place.

"The ditch runs all around the hut like a moat, do you see?" Sonia breathed in Rye's ear. "They must pull in the bridge at night, to keep out bloodhogs and other enemies. Any beast trying to leap the gap would risk falling onto the points of those spears."

Rye nodded grimly. The hut was built of dark stones, but its roof gleamed white. How many bones must it have taken to roof a place of that size? Who were the people who had died to provide those bones? How many Weld volunteers had been among the dead? Were Sholto's bones among the rest?

Dirk had seen the bones, too. His arm had begun to tremble. Or perhaps it was Rye himself who was shaking. He could not be sure.

Linked tightly together, the companions stood and watched as Cap persuaded Bones to drag the sled on over the bridge. They remained motionless as, once Bones was safely out of the way, the end of a folding ladder dropped down through the steam. They waited while a wizened little man wearing a puffy velvet beret climbed down the ladder carrying a flickering lantern. But when Cap and the trader crossed the bridge, three shadows flitted after them.

"The poor fellow grows madder every day," the wizened man rumbled in the deep, rich voice that did not match his appearance at all. He jerked his head at Bones, who was drawing the sled into place in front of the hut. "What's all this about wizards in the Saltings?"

"Oh, just another of his visions," Cap said carelessly. "He spends too much time alone out there. Come and sit by the Soak."

He led the visitor toward the gleam of water, and the two sat down, facing one another with the lantern between them. Rye, Dirk, and Sonia followed.

Close up, the spring was not nearly as inviting as it had looked from a distance. It was little more than a puddle ringed with mud. The people of the Den plainly used the water, however, for a few white bowls lay scattered around the puddle's rim. Rye thought the bowls were ordinary pottery, at first. It took a moment or two for him to realize, with sick horror, that they were made of human skulls.

Instinctively he glanced over his shoulder at Bones. Having placed the sled to his satisfaction, the old man was lowering himself to the ground beside it, his long, skinny limbs folding till he looked like a crouching spider. He was muttering to himself, fumbling with his ghastly necklaces, so that the yellowed teeth clicked against one another like rain pattering on a roof. His stomach heaving, Rye turned back to the two men by the Soak.

"I dislike being called a cheat, Captain," Four-Eyes was saying in injured tones as he settled himself. "My reputation is my livelihood."

"Quite," Cap replied calmly. "So you'd be wise not to take advantage of your best customers. Word gets around, you know. I didn't see the stranger's belongings myself, but it was clear from Bones's description that you didn't pay nearly enough for them. I daresay you kept the best things for yourself and traded the rest on quickly enough. What did you get for them?"

Four-Eyes shrugged, turning down the corners of his mouth. "Oh, very little," he said. "The fellow had fallen into an old jell pit, after all. More things than his neck were broken, and the items that were still whole were in a very sad state indeed I'm afraid."

He sighed gustily. "Still, I made the best of it. I managed to trade the coat, which was not in bad condition, for the sign on my vehicle. Certainly I can't read it myself, but a sign gives a business a professional tone. I've been meaning to have it done ever since I came by the paint a month or two ago."

He glanced across the trench to his wagon with childish satisfaction.

"You've a fine new lantern, too, I see," said Cap, nodding at the lamp burning on the ground between them. "That at least came from the stranger's bag in one piece, did it?"

"Hardly new," the trader murmured, smoothly avoiding the question. "Rather battered, I fear. Still, we must all make do with what we can get, Cap, as you know. Now, about this bloodhog skull . . ."

"Oh, never mind the skull, Four-Eyes," said Cap, smiling. "Clearly it's of no real interest to you, if all you can offer for it is a few shivs of tarny root and a bunch of traveler's weed. We'll just do our usual jell trade, and —"

"Not so fast, my friend!" the trader broke in smoothly. "Nothing would please me more than to do you a favor, and I've been thinking. The next stop on my rounds is the Diggings, and it's occurred to me that one of the guards there might well be interested in a bloodhog skull. So I might just be able to offer you a little more. . . ."

Rye had stopped listening. He was staring at the lantern — the rusty, dented, but suddenly very familiar-looking lantern glowing on the dusty ground. There was a roaring in his ears that drowned out all other sound. He was remembering some words he had read in Sholto's note of farewell to their mother.

I fear my decision will grieve you, so I am going quietly, without fuss. I have taken one of the lanterns. I hope you will not mind this.

His throat aching, Rye struggled to accept what he was seeing. He struggled to accept, at last, that his dream of Sholto had been false, that Sholto was dead.

"We must go!" Sonia hissed suddenly. "The others are coming. We must get back over the bridge before they reach it!"

Rye looked around and saw the people from the mounds trudging along the sled tracks toward the bridge. He knew that Sonia was right. Once everyone was crowded inside the small area bounded by the trench, it would be almost impossible for the three intruders to remain unnoticed. The ghostly shape of the skimmer hook alone would eventually give them away.

And there was no reason to stay, in any case. He had heard enough . . . more than enough.

Dirk seemed to agree, for he turned his back without a word on the two men haggling by the Soak. Dirk's face was drawn. Rye knew that his brother's rage and burning desire for revenge had drained away, leaving only a terrible sadness behind.

Sholto had not been struck down by human hands. The treacherous ground of the Scour had killed him.

Certainly, Bones had robbed his body before carrying it back to the Saltings so that the snails could reduce it to a skeleton. No doubt that was why Cap had been so anxious to stop Rye, Dirk, and Sonia from finding out about the death. He had feared their anger — feared they would use their magic to attack the people of the Den in revenge for what Bones had done.

But what point was there in anger? Sholto himself, with his cold, clear way of looking at things, would have understood Bones's actions perfectly. He would have agreed that life here was too hard for anything to be wasted — even a dead man's bones.

As quickly and silently as they could, the three companions moved back to the bridge and crept across it. Bones was still mumbling over his beads by the hut. Rye hoped fervently that the old man would not look up. If he did, he would surely see the misty shape of the giant hook floating over the trench. But Bones did not stir.

The people from the mounds were very close now, plodding along with bowed heads, most carrying skull bowls partly filled with bloodred jell. Reaching the end of the bridge, the companions just had time to slip around to the far side of the monstrous wagon before Floss, Needle, and the rest began slowly filing past.

The wagon looked even larger close up. Warmth radiated from its metal surfaces, and it was still wreathed in a moist, foul-smelling haze.

Rye gazed at it, wondering dully how it moved without beasts to pull it. He bent to look at the vehicle's underside, and as he did, he caught sight of a strange little circular design painted low down on the side panel just below the doorway.

Rye peered at the design. It was hard to see clearly because it was a dark color — red, he thought. It did not look as if it had been painted with a brush, but rather as if it had been hastily scrawled with a fingertip.

He was just about to point it out to Dirk and Sonia when without warning Dirk pulled himself up into the wagon, pushing aside the flap of goat hide that served as a door.

"Dirk!" Rye whispered in panic, pushing back the hood so his brother could see him. "What are you doing?"

Dirk looked back over his shoulder. "What do you think?" he muttered. "The trader said his next stop was the Diggings. That is on our way, and it will be far safer and faster for us to ride with him than to walk. If he does the same thing there as he has done here, we will easily be able to slip out of the wagon while he is trading."

"But —"

Dirk's face was very hard. "If we ask that little worm to help us, he will certainly refuse or ask a price we cannot afford to pay. So we will take what we want without his knowledge. He plainly did well out of Sholto's death, so he can help us continue Sholto's quest. Stop shilly-shallying, Rye! Come on!"

He turned away, the goat hide falling back into place behind him.

THE STOWAWAYS

S onia sighed. "This is what happens when you travel with heroes," she murmured. "How they love to take risks!" Her words were mocking, but her eyes were dark with sympathy. It was as if she knew as well as Rye did that Dirk's need to do something — anything — to smother his grief over Sholto's death had made him seize upon the idea of hiding in the trader's wagon.

"But in fact Dirk is right," she added, after a moment's thought. "While he carries that metal hook, the hood, the shell, and the speed ring will not work as well as they should. We might be taking a risk stealing a ride, but it is a smaller risk than making the journey on foot."

"I doubt there is any point in making the journey at all," Rye said through stiff lips. "We no longer have any reason to believe that the one they call the Master is the Enemy sending the skimmers to Weld."

"But, Rye —"

"We thought my dream of Sholto was proof that the skimmers were here," Rye went on doggedly. "But the dream meant nothing. Sholto was never in a red place. He was in the Saltings. Then he was in the Scour. And then he was . . . gone."

He could not say "dead." He could not bring himself to say the word.

"My dreams of Dirk were true," he mumbled, feeling as if the words were being dragged from him one by one. "I thought it was the same for Sholto."

He felt Sonia touch his arm and swallowed desperately to stop himself from breaking down. It had meant so much to him to believe that he had a special bond with both his lost brothers — a bond that could help save them.

"I am sure the dream did not mean nothing, Rye," Sonia said quietly. "You have a gift. At times — at certain times — you can reach out to people you care for. And I have been wondering . . ."

She hesitated, then her hand tightened on his arm and she hurried on. "We know from the fragments of journal we found that Sholto had begun to — to see things that were not real. Could it be that in the dream, your mind and his were linked so closely that you were sharing one of his visions?"

Understanding came to Rye on a wave of pain.

Yes, that explained it all. He had been sharing a delirious vision — the vision, perhaps, that had come to Sholto as he lay dying in the abandoned jell pit. It was no more based on fact than Sholto's ravings of enemies who drugged his drinking water.

That would account for the fact that in the dream of the red place the skimmers menaced Sholto but never reached him. The skimmers had been illusions, like the dead skimmers of his journal notes.

Rye leaned against the wagon and closed his eyes. The rusty metal was warm against his cheek. Gradually his pain eased, and a strange sort of comfort took its place. Perhaps he had been wrong about what the dream of the red place meant, but he had been with Sholto all the same.

And Sholto seemed very close to him now. Perhaps, Rye thought slowly, that was because the wagon had once held Sholto's possessions. Or perhaps it was just because Rye knew it had, and his imagination was doing the rest.

"We missed him by so little," he murmured. "I knew, when we left Fleet, that time was short. But I had no idea how short."

An image of Sholto's lantern burning on alien ground floated into his mind. And with it, quite suddenly, came the knowledge that Sholto would not have despaired at this moment. He would have put his feelings aside and turned the cool light of his reason on the situation.

Rye did his best to do the same, and the mists that had clouded his mind cleared a little. He sighed and opened his eyes to find Sonia watching him anxiously.

"I am sorry," he said. "Of course the Master could still be the Enemy of Weld. We have no proof that he is, but we have no proof that he is not, either. And of course we must find out one way or the other."

The girl nodded wordlessly.

"And of course Dirk is right about hiding in the wagon," Rye went on. "It is what Sholto would have done also, if he had had the chance."

It was more difficult for Rye and Sonia to clamber up into the wagon than it had been for the taller Dirk, but they managed it. In moments, they were crawling into steamy, strong-smelling dimness, with the hide curtain flapping down behind them.

"At last!" Dirk's voice hissed from the shadows.

Rye's elbow struck something hard, and he grunted with pain. Reflecting ruefully that the armor shell protected him from attack but not from his own clumsiness, he turned to see what had hurt him.

It was a bulky metal box with a padlocked lid. The box was bolted to the floor beside the driver's seat, and very near its base, there was another of the curious little painted designs.

It had clearly been daubed by the same hand as the design on the outside of the wagon, but this time, the spots and crosses were enclosed in a square instead of a circle.

"Look at this," Rye whispered to Sonia, pointing at the mark. "There was something like it outside, too. Could it be some sort of protection charm?"

"If it is, Four-Eyes has little faith in it, since he feels he needs to protect the box with bolts and a padlock as well," Sonia answered dryly.

"It is the slimy cheat's cashbox, no doubt," Dirk said, overhearing. "Do not touch it."

"It is too big to be a cashbox," Sonia objected, but this time Dirk did not bother to reply.

Rubbing his elbow, Rye sat back on his heels and looked around.

The driver's seat was like a throne, very large and padded with goat hides. Squarely in front of it, a metal wheel sprouted like a giant daisy from a pole sticking up through the floor. A window gave a clear view of the way ahead, and below the window was a metal panel studded with levers, knobs, and a large dial like a clock face with only one hand.

The shadowy storage area behind the seat was packed to the roof with barrels, lumpy sacks, yellowed bones, bundles of ragged garments, and baskets overflowing with everything from old boots to digging tools. Hunched over to avoid hitting his head on the roof, Dirk was fossicking in one of the baskets.

"I thought some of Sholto's things might still be here, but so far I have found nothing I recognize," he said. "Not that it is easy to find anything in this jumble."

"Look at all this food!" Sonia said indignantly, prodding a bulging sack that smelled strongly of onions. "And Four-Eyes said his supplies were low! He is a cheat and a liar, just as Bones said."

As if to prove her point, the trader's voice boomed out on the other side of the trench. "Well, my friends, I fear your scourings don't amount to very much this time. Two shivs of tarny roots I'll give for the lot, and that's generous."

"*Generous?*" a woman cried shrilly. "It's robbery!"

There was a chorus of angry jeers.

"It's not my fault that times are hard, my friends!" Four-Eyes called in an injured voice. "I'm doing the best I can for you. Nanny's Pride farm is the last stop before I reach here, as you know. The good folk there assured me that the tarny roots in the sacks they gave me were pulled only this morning. You won't get fresher!"

"Fresh or wilted, tarny roots all taste like horse feed to me," another voice grumbled. "Didn't you get any salted meat from Nanny's Pride, Four-Eyes?"

"Very little," sighed Four-Eyes. "They're struggling to produce anything but tarny roots since so many of their people were taken for the Diggings."

Rye crawled to the doorway beside the driver's seat, pushed the goat hide flap a little aside and cautiously peeped out.

The area between the hut and the Soak was crowded with the people from the mounds, and torches now burned in several places. The trader was still sitting opposite Cap with his back to the wagon. But he had removed the velvet beret from his head, and gleaming in the back of his hairless skull were two staring eyes.

Rye's stomach turned over. "The trader has eyes in the back of his head!" he hissed.

"What?" demanded Dirk from the back of the wagon. "Do you mean —?"

"I mean what I say!" hissed Rye. "The trader has an extra pair of eyes — I can see them!"

Sonia squeaked in horror.

"Rye, get away from there!" Dirk snapped, sounding very rattled. "You are not wearing the hood, remember!"

"Yes, Rye, come on!" Sonia whispered, beginning to edge between the towering stacks of goods.

As Rye turned from the doorway, there was a high, chittering sound right beside him. He jumped, then sighed with relief as a small pink nose poked inquisitively from beneath the driver's seat.

"A clink!" he exclaimed.

"Keep your voice down!" Dirk growled. "And leave the clink alone! Four-Eyes keeps it to catch mice, I daresay."

As they did in Fleet, Rye thought, remembering the little creature he had seen in the fireplace of the Fleet guesthouse.

Olt's men had killed that clink — killed it for no reason except pure, bullying spite. Wincing at the memory, Rye dug into his pocket and pulled out a handful of hoji nuts left over from the uncomfortable meal in the Saltings. The pink nose twitched, and the clink chattered excitedly.

"Do not feed it, Rye," Dirk warned, alerted by the sound. "If you do, it will come after you, begging for more, and give us away. Clinks are never satisfied."

Rye hurriedly pushed the nuts back into his pocket. With a disappointed snuffle, the clink vanished beneath the seat again.

"Oh!" Sonia exclaimed. "Look at this!"

Wondering what she had found, Rye sidled through the piles of goods till he reached the back of the wagon.

He found Dirk and Sonia crouching by the rear wall on a tangle of empty sacks. They were peering into a large box that had been wedged into a corner. The box had wire mesh at the top, and inside were a pair of fine ducks and six downy ducklings, snugly nestled in a bed of straw.

"We will put the cage by the bridge, where it will be quickly seen," Dirk was saying excitedly. "It will seem that it has appeared by magic!"

"Yes!" Sonia hissed gleefully. "And Four-Eyes can hardly claim the ducks are his. He swore he had nothing of value to trade."

Dirk grinned up at Rye, his eyes sparkling. "By the Wall, just think what this will mean to Cap's people, Rye! If they tend these birds well, in time they will have a whole flock! They will have fresh eggs every day, as we did at home."

Rye gazed down at the family of ducks sleeping with their heads under their wings. How long ago it seemed since he, Dirk, Sholto, and their mother had sat around the table in the little house in Southwall, talking in low voices and eating the cold food that was all they could risk at night in skimmer season.

He remembered Sholto peeling the shell from a hard-boiled duck egg and saying the words that had haunted him ever since.

For skimmers, Weld may be nothing but a giant feeding bowl, in which tender prey are conveniently trapped.

Life is very hard for the poor souls of the Den, Rye thought. But the night skies at least are safe. If there are skimmers in this place, they go to Weld to feed.

And that is why you are here. Remember why you are here!

Rye stiffened. It was as if Sholto had whispered in his ear.

"If we do as you say, we can forget traveling to the Master's headquarters quickly and in secrecy," he said in a level voice. "Four-Eyes will know someone has been in his wagon. He will search it from end to end. Nothing is more certain."

Dirk hesitated, the excitement slowly fading from his face.

"But, Rye, do you not want to help Bones and his people?" Sonia demanded passionately.

"Yes," Rye said. "But we are here to find the source of the skimmers. We should not lose sight of that goal. We should not —"

"Not allow ourselves to be drawn into struggles that do not concern us," Dirk finished flatly. "As I did, beyond the golden Door."

"Dirk, I did not say that!" Rye felt his face grow hot.

Dirk regarded him quizzically. "Perhaps not, little brother, but it is true. And I was about to do the same thing again. Of course you are right. Cap and his tribe will have to do without our help for now."

Sonia was frowning and biting her lip. Rye wondered if she knew how hard it had been for him to say what he had — if she knew how it would have thrilled him to put the ducks into the hands of Bones and the other people of the Den.

Whether she did or not, she did not argue. Casting a last regretful look at the cage, she seized a few of the empty sacks and began to drag them to the other back corner of the wagon, wrinkling her nose at the smells of onions, salted fish, and goat that rose from the coarse fabric as it was moved.

"Ho, Cap!" Rye heard Bones shout. "Where be the magic ones? They be a match for cheating ol' Four-Eyes, them three!"

"They've gone, you buffoon!" a high jeering voice shrieked. "As soon as they got rid of you, they —"

"Needle, hold your tongue!" Cap thundered. But the damage was done.

"Why, Cap!" cried Four-Eyes with obvious relish. "I thought you said —"

"Gone?" roared Bones at the same moment. "Gone an' left us?" And he began to howl like a beast.

The piteous sound pierced Rye's heart. He covered his ears, but he could not escape it.

The howling still had not stopped when Four-Eyes strode back to the wagon in triumph. Scourers trailed behind him, carrying the jell and the bloodhog skull he had traded for a sack of tarny roots, some salted goat meat, a bunch of traveler's weed, and a promise to keep silent about the Den's vanished visitors.

It went on while Rye, Sonia, and Dirk, huddled in hiding, heard the hiss of steam, and felt the wagon floor shuddering beneath them as the monstrous vehicle began to move.

And it was still ringing in their ears as the wagon puffed away from the Den and turned onto the track to the Diggings, carrying them with it.

ON THE ROAD

T he trader roared with laughter. "So what do you say to all that?" he boomed over the chugging roar of the wagon. "Suspicious strangers in the Den, and Cap willing to do anything to keep the story quiet! On the very day that old Bones drags home the finest bloodhog skull I've ever seen! What a piece of luck!"

Rye, Sonia, and Dirk tensed in their dark corner. Who was the man talking to?

Rye felt for the crystal in the bag around his neck. Masking the crystal's light carefully with his fingers, he pressed it against the pile of sacks rising in front of him.

A window appeared around the crystal, and there was Four-Eyes sitting in his throne-like seat. He was quite alone. His shoulders were shaking. The eyes in the back of his head streamed with tears of laughter.

A shiver ran down Rye's spine.

"A smoked whine, my dear?" the man chortled at last, mopping his face with a purple silk handkerchief, then reaching around to dab at the second pair of eyes as well. "Why not? We're celebrating!"

He dug into a bag on his lap and dropped something spiky onto the floor by the padlocked metal box. There was an excited chittering sound, a twitching nose appeared from behind the box, and the scrap was snatched away. There was the sound of ravenous crunching.

"He is talking to his clink!" Rye whispered, and heard Sonia and Dirk, who by now were both looking over his shoulder, breathe out in relief.

"I agree with you, Snaffle dear!" Four-Eyes cried merrily. "Your master is a genius! We'll be able to trade that skull for a fortune at the Diggings! Not to mention that we still have those ducks in the back. Should we offer them to the Diggings guards as well?"

The nose reappeared at the box's corner, and the clink gave a squeak.

"You're quite right, of course!" Four-Eyes nodded. "They'd only eat them — feathers and all, most likely — which would be a pity, in some ways. Still, Snaffle my dear, we must be practical. Who else would have the means to pay us so much?"

Rye felt Sonia stiffen and heard Dirk swear under his breath. He gritted his teeth, trying not to think of Bones, and Bones's great hopes for the three "magic ones" who had brought him nothing but grief.

The trader wriggled in his seat, arching his back as if to ease aching muscles. The clink chattered, and again Four-Eyes nodded as if he understood exactly what it was saying.

"Just a slight cramp — nothing to worry about, my dear. But I'm tired, I admit. I sometimes wonder if I'm getting too old for this business. Still, the skull was worth it."

He took his left hand from the wheel and tapped the metal box with satisfaction. "Not to mention that the Den scourings brought the jell in our crock right up to the brim! That will please them at the Diggings. Especially now, when I hear . . ."

He leaned slightly toward the clink and lowered his voice as if speaking to it in confidence. Rye had to strain to hear him. "Especially now, Snaffle, when I hear whisperings that something big is about to happen at the Harbor. Something *rather* important to the Master, I gather, and therefore not on any account to fail. But hush! Not a word!"

He began to raise a finger to his lips but stopped midway, put his head on one side, and stroked his chin instead.

The clink snuffled.

"That's just what I was thinking," Four-Eyes murmured. "Mysterious strangers in the Scour . . . and so-called wizards appearing in the Saltings . . . It could be chance, but it could also be connected with the rumors about the Harbor. The Master has his enemies, we all know that. Which means, Snaffle . . ."

He hunched forward, tapping the wheel with his fingertips. The eyes in the back of his head rolled upward till only the whites showed. The sight was so horrible that Rye had to bite his lips to stop himself from exclaiming in disgust.

"Which means," Four-Eyes went on slowly, "that the Master's people would pay very well to hear what I've sworn to keep secret."

Absentmindedly he tossed a second smoked whine to the clink and popped one into his own mouth as well.

"Really most unfortunate," he mumbled, chewing rapidly. "I should have thought of it before. Oh, now I've given myself a headache!"

He groaned and rubbed his forehead. "Most unfortunate," he repeated. "But bargains are bargains. There's no going back on them, Snaffle. Sharp trading is one thing, but my word is my bond."

He bent over the wheel, staring pensively at the smoke puffing from his vehicle's funnel. Slowly the eyes in the back of his head returned to normal.

"And on second thoughts, my pet," he murmured, plucking a fragment of whine wing from his bottom lip, "it might be just as well if we know nothing about events that concern the Master. In fact, to be on the safe side, we might take a little holiday after this run — get ourselves out of the way for a few weeks, till the Harbor affair is settled one way or another. What do you say?"

Tiny claws scrabbled on the wagon floor, and the clink chirruped.

"I'm glad you agree, my dear," Four-Eyes said tenderly. "No, don't ask me for any more treats. Smoked whines are very salty. Next you'll be wanting a drink, and we need every drop of our water for the engine. Why don't you get some sleep while you can? I'll relax, too. Diggings in two hours."

He settled himself more comfortably in his seat and began to hum tunelessly. Slowly the eyes in the back of his head closed.

Rye returned the crystal to the little brown bag and turned to his companions.

Sonia's face was so pale that it glimmered in the dimness like an oval of floating white smoke. Without a word, she slumped back on the heap of empty sacks, looking completely exhausted.

But Rye and Dirk, once they had settled down beside her, were too full of what they had heard to keep silent. They began at once to whisper to each other, confident that the humming trader would not hear them over the chugging and rattling of the wagon.

"If Olt's brother is the one sending the skimmers to Weld, this big event the trader spoke of could be some new plan of attack," said Rye.

Dirk grimaced. "It could be. We will find out soon enough. The thing I would like to know is why jell is so precious here. By the Wall, the trader keeps it in that locked box, as if it was gold! But jell is nothing! Its only use is as a dye, and a very little goes a long way."

"A dye for cloth, you mean?" Sonia murmured.

"Yes, and a very cheap, common dye at that," said Dirk, turning to look at her. "Why do you think the Keep soldiers' leggings are red? Or the Keep orphans' uniforms, come to that?"

"Olt's flags and banners were red, too," Rye put in.

"Of course." Dirk shrugged. "There is jell in plenty in the west. While I was staying in Fleet, I often saw workers come across it when they were digging deep."

Sonia blinked at him sleepily. "So in Weld, and in the west of Dorne, jell is not highly valued because it is plentiful and used only to dye cloth. But here it is very highly valued, so it is either not so plentiful — which does not seem to be the case — or it is used for something else."

"I cannot think what," Dirk said, shaking his head. "You cannot eat jell, or build with it, or use it as fuel — all those things, and dozens of others, have been tried."

"Yet the Master wants every scrap he can get," Rye said. "He must have discovered another use for it!"

"Then he has succeeded where thousands before him have failed," Dirk muttered. "By the Wall, it is a mystery! I would love to know the truth of it."

"No doubt we will, when we reach the Harbor," Rye said uneasily.

Sonia yawned. Her eyelids were drooping. Framed by her close-fitting cap, her face looked small and pinched. "I am sorry," she mumbled. "I am . . . so tired. I don't recall ever having been so tired in my whole life before."

"It is all that thinking, Sonia!" Dirk teased gently, and Rye noted with surprise that there was real affection in his brother's voice. It seemed that Sonia's eager support of the plan to steal the ducks had made Dirk think of her as a friend at last, instead of as a nuisance.

"In fact, we should all get some rest," Dirk went on. "The sound of the wagon slowing and stopping · will wake us when we reach the Diggings."

Rye leaned back against the pile of smelly sacks. It was exquisite relief to close his eyes. He was just drifting deliciously into sleep when he felt a tickling sensation on the tip of his little finger. He woke with a start, realizing that the armor shell was slowly sliding off.

He caught the shell just in time to stop it falling to the ground and held it tightly, appalled at his own carelessness. He had become so used to the shell that he had almost forgotten he was wearing it. But as he had begun falling asleep, it had sensed that he felt safe — safe for the first time since the attack of the giant bird — and it had loosened accordingly.

Vowing to take more care in future, Rye pushed the shell back into the little bag hanging around his neck. After a moment's thought, he took off the speed ring and added it to the bag as well, just to be on the safe side.

As he lay back again, his hand curved protectively over the bag, he reminded himself that he had still not discovered the purpose of two of the powers inside it. The crystal, the ring, the hood, the serpent scale, the red feather, and the snail shell had all revealed their strengths. But the paper-wrapped sweet and the tiny key remained mysteries.

And what of the ninth power?

Nine powers to aid you in your quest . . .

But there were only eight objects in the bag. Sonia was convinced that the Fellan Edelle had meant that the crystal possessed two powers — the power to light the darkness and the power to see through solid objects. Yet for some reason this answer did not quite satisfy Rye.

He closed his eyes, letting his thoughts wander. The wagon ground on along the track, shuddering and roaring like a beast. A memory of riding to Fleet in FitzFee's cart slid into Rye's mind. The only sounds on that journey beyond the golden Door had been the clip-clopping of the old mare's hooves on the road and the sound of FitzFee and his little daughter singing. It had been far more pleasant than this.

Dirk and Sonia were already asleep, and despite the noise of the wagon, the prickliness of the sacks at his back and the loud, monotonous humming of the trader at the wheel, Rye soon joined them.

They slept the sleep of exhaustion and relief, secure in the knowledge that hours must pass before they would have to wake.

They did not hear the soft rasping as four lumpy sacks labeled "Nanny's Pride Tarny Roots" were slit open from the inside. They did not hear the tiny sounds of four small, chunky figures sliding out of their long confinement, standing up in the darkness, and stretching cramped limbs.

They did not hear Four-Eyes the trader's brief struggle as a white pad reeking of something sweet was clapped over his mouth and nose from behind. And they did not stir as one of the small figures took the wheel of the wagon while Four-Eyes's slumped body was dragged from the driver's seat.

It all happened in moments. The noises of the wagon did not alter. Snaffle the clink, fast asleep behind the metal box, did not stir.

And so it was that when strong hands seized Rye, Sonia, and Dirk, they were taken completely by surprise.

BIRD, BEAN, CHUB, AND ITCH

R ye had been dreaming of Bones when he woke
to terror. Dazed, still haunted by the image
of Bones howling at the lowering sky, he at
first could not believe that he was really feeling the
knifepoint grazing his throat. There was a strange,
sickly sweet smell in the air. It made his head spin.

The wagon slowed and stopped, its roar giving
way to a sullen hissing. Rye tried to move and instantly
an arm tightened around his shoulders.

"Do not stir!" a harsh female voice rasped in his
ear. "Sit like a rock if you value your life."

"Shall I throw Four-Eyes out, Bird?" a man
growled from the front of the wagon.

"No, Bean!" Rye's captor barked. "We might need
him yet. Stay at the wheel and keep the fire stoked. We
won't be stopping for long."

So the trader's wagon had been taken over. Rye

hoped desperately that the invaders were starving scourers bent on stealing Four-Eyes's stock. If that was it, he, Sonia, and Dirk had a chance.

But what if the Master had somehow found out that three strangers from the Saltings were aboard the wagon? What if the invaders were soldiers, sent to take them prisoner?

Rye could not turn to look at Dirk, but Sonia's face was swimming in the dimness straight ahead of him. A bearded man squatted behind her, holding her tightly. The blade of a bone knife gleamed at her throat.

Sonia's eyes were huge with fear. Her lips were slightly parted. She was staring at Rye's neck — at the knifepoint hovering under his chin.

The woman called Bird moved uneasily. "Shut your witch's eyes!" she hissed at Sonia. "Shut them or your friend here will regret it!"

She moved the knifepoint a fraction. Sonia hastily did as she was told.

Rye thought of the little brown bag of powers. It was there, lying against his chest, under his shirt, well below his captor's arm. If only he could get to it — get his hands on the armor shell! But the black eyes of Sonia's captor were fixed on him, watching for the slightest movement.

"Chub!" Bird snapped. "Is the big one safe yet?"

"Yes," a frightened female voice replied from behind them. "But he only stopped struggling just now, Bird. He's strong as a bloodhog!"

"Come and see to the witch," Bird ordered. "Make haste!"

The sickly sweet smell suddenly became much stronger as a dark-clad figure carrying a pad of white cloth moved in front of Rye and bent over Sonia.

With a choking cry, Rye tried to hurl himself forward, but Bird was ready for him. She held him with a grip of iron, and her knife hand remained steady.

"Do that again and you'll cut your own throat," she snarled. "The witch hasn't been harmed. Myrmon isn't a poison. It'll make her sleep, that's all."

The dark figure straightened. As it sidled out of the way, Rye saw that Sonia had slumped sideways, and that her bearded captor was easing her down onto the floor.

"That will put a stop to her mischief," Bird said fiercely.

"She . . . is not a witch!" panted Rye. He could feel blood running down his neck and realized that the knife had pierced his skin. He could not have cared less.

Bird snorted. "So you say. But I've got eyes in my head, and ears as well. You're the three Bones of the Den called magic, and I'd believe Bones a thousand times over before I'd believe you. Folk call him mad, but they forget how he fought the Master in his time. My old granny doesn't forget, though. She's told us of those days often."

So the invaders were not soldiers. They were against the Master, not for him!

"We — we are no friends of the Master, Bird," Rye burst out. "We are your allies! Let us go! Steal what you like from the trader's wagon — we will never tell a soul, I swear!"

It was as if he had not spoken. "Itch, help Chub drag the giant out," Bird said to the man crouching beside Sonia. "Then Bean can get us moving again."

They were going to leave Dirk, drugged and helpless, alone in the Scour!

"No!" Rye begged. "Please —"

"Quiet!" Bird snapped.

As Itch crawled to his feet, Rye realized with a shock that he was very short indeed — no taller than a Weld child of eight or nine. In fact, he looked like FitzFee! He had the same strong build. He even carried a heavy bow on his belt, as FitzFee did.

And Chub, the wielder of the reeking white cloth, might well be just like him, Rye realized now. Chub had also seemed short, but at the time, Rye had been too afraid for Sonia to think about what that might mean.

Rye's heart leaped. Could it be that Itch and Chub were related to FitzFee? Were they cousins, perhaps, who had fled to the east to escape Olt? If so . . .

He decided to take a chance. "Does the name FitzFee mean anything to you?" he asked loudly.

Itch's face went blank. Rye felt Bird stiffen in shock, and heard Chub gasp loudly in the shadows to his right. Plainly they all recognized the name. Hope flared in him.

"FitzFee is our friend," he hurried on. "FitzFee would tell you —"

"Hold your tongue or lose it, sorcerer!" Bird burst out, her voice shaking. "We know your tricks!"

Rye froze. What had happened? What had he done? His captor was panting. Her hand was trembling, and the knifepoint was scratching Rye's skin, stinging and burning.

"Go, Itch!" Bird ordered. "I can deal with him."

"Bird, there *is* a cage of ducks here, just like they said!" Chub squeaked from the other side of the wagon. "Live ducks! Six of them!"

Rye felt Bird tense, but she did not hesitate. "It can't be helped," she snapped. "Put them out with the giant. And get rid of that pad of myrmon, Chub, for pity's sake! You'll have us all fainting, next."

Silently, Itch moved out of Rye's view. *Now!* Rye thought. Very slowly, concentrating on not moving his shoulders, he began to edge his hand up toward the little brown bag.

He heard bumping and panting as Chub and Itch heaved boxes and sacks out onto the track to clear a path, then dragged Dirk's body away. A few moments later, feet came padding back and there was a scraping sound as the duck cage was moved and lifted. The ducks quacked sleepily as they, too, were carried out.

Bird's hand had stopped trembling but she was still breathing rapidly, and her body was rigid with tension. With agonizing slowness, Rye moved his fingers upward.

"Ready, Bean!" he heard Chub call.

With a clank, a hiss, and a creak, the wagon began to move, very slowly at first and then a little faster. Pebbles shifted and cracked under the mighty rollers. The puffing, roaring sound began. The speed increased. The metal walls rattled, and the floor began to vibrate.

Bird breathed out. Her body relaxed a little. Plainly she had feared that Bean would not be able to make the monstrous vehicle start again. Rye gave a little grunt and lurched very slightly, as if the shuddering of the wagon had thrown him off balance. At the same time, he slid his hand up and pushed it inside his shirt so that the bag of powers was under his fingers.

"Good work, Bean!" Bird shouted over the noise of the wagon. "Now, Chub and Itch, clear everything else out! Everything but the jell safe and that black coat and cap I chose before."

"There's some g-good stuff here, B-Bird!" a male voice with a slight stammer complained. *Itch*, Rye thought, trying to loosen the neck of the little bag with his fingertips.

"Yes, Bird!" Chub cried shrilly. "Some of our own good tarny roots and goat meat, for a start! And the biggest bloodhog skull you've ever —"

"Keep your minds on what we're doing, for pity's sake!" Bird shouted, her voice sharp with irritation. "The wagon's got to look the part or they'll get suspicious. The plan's risky enough as it is!"

Chub and Itch made no more protests. Fresh air, dust, and steam wafted into the wagon as the hide curtain was pulled aside. Rattling, dragging sounds began, followed by dull thuds as goods were tossed out of the open doorway onto the side of the track.

Rye had managed to get the tip of one finger through the neck of the bag. He held his breath and pushed deeper, feeling for the armor shell.

And suddenly the front of his shirt lit up like a lantern! His finger had touched the light crystal, and the crystal had responded instantly. Even muffled by the fabric of the bag, its beam was startlingly bright in the dimness.

Rye jerked his hand back, but it was too late. Bird's yell of shock was already ringing in his ears. Appalled, he heard Chub and Itch come running and heard Bean bellowing questions from the driver's seat. He heard Bird gabbling orders, felt his arms caught and held. He felt Bird drag the little brown bag from under his shirt and with a snarl of disgust wrench it from his neck, snapping the red cord in two.

The next moment, the woman was pounding toward the front of the wagon, and it was Itch who was dragging back his head and threatening him with the knife. Then Bird was back, planting herself in front of Rye so that he saw her for the first time.

She was shorter than Itch and Chub, with powerful shoulders and a mass of tightly curling brown hair. Her square, determined face was bleached and sweating, and she was rubbing the palms of her hands on her black goatskin jacket as if she had been touching something poisonous or disgusting.

"There, the foul thing has gone," she panted.

"*No!*" Rye barely recognized his own voice as the word burst from his lips.

As Bird grinned, gleeful at his dismay, white-hot anger blazed through him. "You stupid, grinning barbarian!" he shouted. "Do you know what you have done? You have thrown away your one chance of freedom from the Master!"

With fierce, pointless satisfaction, he saw the woman's face twitch and the grin fade.

"We were no threat to you!" he raged on. "But you left my brother, drugged and helpless, in the Scour. And now you have robbed me of the only means I had to get back to him in time to save him!"

Hot tears were spilling from his eyes and running down his cheeks. Furiously he dashed them away.

Bird wiped the sweat from her brow with the back of her hand and exchanged glances with the silent Chub and Itch.

"Finish clearing the wagon," she ordered.

"But, Bird —" Rye heard Chub say doubtfully.

"Go!" Bird snapped. "I'll be in no danger. Look at him! Now that his sorcerer's bag of tricks has gone, he's nothing but a blubbering boy."

Nothing she said could have dried Rye's tears more quickly. At that moment, he felt such hatred for her that he could have lunged forward and strangled her with his bare hands.

Perhaps she saw this in his eyes, for as Itch released him she quickly crouched by Sonia's side, the knife in her hand.

"Touch me and the witch dies," she said evenly.

Rye's rage flickered and burned out, leaving him cold as ashes. He set his lips, and nodded.

"Listen to me, Spy," Bird said, looking straight into his eyes. "It's not our fault that you chose to stow away in Four-Eyes's wagon tonight. We were already here when you came. Our plan was under way, and there was no turning back for us. We had no reason to trust you and couldn't risk your interference. We did what we had to do."

Rye kept silent. Did the woman think he was going to agree with her? Over the chugging of the wagon, he could hear Chub and Itch disposing of the last of the trader's stock. *So much food*, he thought. *Enough to keep the people of the Den for a year or more.*

"You have lost a brother, but so have Bean and I," Bird went on evenly. "Two weeks ago, Bell was taken as a slave to the Diggings. Chub's husband and Itch's twin sisters were taken also, and sixteen others of our clan. Today we received their message telling us where in the Diggings they were. Tonight we are going to get them back."

Rye felt a flicker of unwilling sympathy. He fought it down.

"We were going to put all three of you out of the wagon, but when I saw you, I realized we could use you," Bird said. "If you agree to help us and our plan succeeds, you will be back with your brother before dawn."

"By then he will be dead," Rye answered, his lips barely moving. "A bloodhog will have taken him."

"Possibly," Bird agreed coolly. "But bloodhogs aren't as common as they once were. It's more likely that he will be lying exactly where we left him — thirsty and sore, but alive. We'll give you food and water, then you can go your way and we'll go ours."

"And if I don't agree to help you?"

"Then I'll kill the witch before your eyes and then kill you."

Rye stared at her. She returned his gaze unflinchingly.

He found himself doubting that she would carry out her threat. He was almost sure she would not. But he knew he could not take the risk. Bird was desperate. It seemed to him that even she did not know what she would do if he refused her.

"Very well," he said. "What do you want me to do?"

THE DIGGINGS

Rye saw the Diggings long before the wagon reached it. Light thick with smoke and dust filled the horizon to the right of the track, crawling upward to meet the clouds, oozing through the wire mesh of a high fence like soup through a strainer to pool on the tortured earth of the Scour.

And there was sound. The Diggings never slept, it seemed. From where he sat, perched on the jell safe beside the silent Bean, Rye could at first hear only a dull, pulsing clamor. Then he began to pick out individual sounds — the clanging of metal on rock, the rumbling of wheels, the roaring of rough voices, the cracking of whips.

His mouth grew dry. He shifted awkwardly on the hard metal box, trying to calm himself. The long, dark coat Bird had made him put on was buttoned stiffly to his chin. His hair was covered by a close-fitting black cap that prickled his scalp. In his hand was a note written on thick gray paper and bearing the symbol he had first seen on the sign at the edge of the Saltings: the mark of the Master.

"Bell and the others were not taken without a fight," Bird had said grimly as she handed the paper to him. "It was a fight we had no chance of winning, but at least this came out of it. The slave hunter in charge of the pack that invaded the farm must have dropped it in the scuffle before we were quelled. It is the cornerstone of our plan. It will persuade the guards to release our people to us."

Her mouth had twisted wryly. "Release our people to *you*, that is. The guards would never believe that farm rats, as they call us, would be sent on such a mission. We were going to force Four-Eyes to do the talking, but as a stranger to the guards, you will be far more convincing."

Rye tossed a hoji nut to the clink chattering in the shadows at his feet. The little creature had come begging the moment he sat down. He had been feeding it ever since, for what did its greed matter now?

"Do not hurt it!" he had burst out when he saw Bird frowning at the pink nose poking hopefully around the corner of the jell safe.

"I wouldn't harm a clink!" Bird had exclaimed. "What do you think I am?"

A savage, Rye had retorted in his mind. *A barbarian!* Yet he knew it was not as simple as that. Bird was the leader of a desperate mission. Dirk had suffered at her hands, but Dirk might well have acted just as ruthlessly if he had been in her place. *Perhaps*, Rye thought uneasily, *even I might have done so. Just a few days ago, it would have been impossible for me, but not now.*

The world outside the Wall had changed him. Just as, according to Annocki, it had changed Sonia. Annocki had said Sonia seemed "more alive" after her time beyond the golden Door.

She would not say the same now, Rye thought grimly, glancing at Sonia lying huddled on the floor of the empty wagon with Bird, Itch, and Chub crouching beside her.

Sonia had fared better than Four-Eyes who, after being given another whiff of myrmon, had been stuffed into a sack and now lay hidden behind his captors. But this was only because Bird wanted Sonia under her hand, in case Rye was at the last moment tempted to betray them.

The light of the Diggings was glaring now. The corner of the fence was very near. Not far past it, a pair of tall mesh gates flanked by large, white-painted marker stones faced the track. There was a notice on one of the gates, but Rye could not make out what it said.

Trying to calm himself, he looked down at the note in his hand and read it for what must have been the twentieth time.

> KYTE—
> DUE TO A CAVE-IN, TWENTY
> (20) FRESH MINE RATS*
> ARE REQUIRED AT THE
> DIGGINGS. SEE TO IT
> WITHOUT DELAY.
>
> *Brand*
>
> <u>* FROM TUNNEL 12, HUT 16</u>

"Itch added what was needed," Bird had said, pointing a stubby finger at the last line. "He's an artist and good at copying. The forgery isn't perfect — we couldn't quite match the ink — but it should do."

Rye had frowned in confusion. "But this says nothing about releasing —"

"That doesn't matter. The only things that matter are the paper and the signature. At this time of night, there'll be no one in authority at the Diggings who can read. The guards can recognize numbers, but that's all."

"Who is Brand? Is he the —?"

"Don't pretend ignorance, Spy!" Bird had hissed. "The time for foolery is long past. Now, do you remember what you have to say?"

Rye did. He had repeated it so often that it was burned into his brain. But Bird would give him no peace until he had repeated it one more time.

"They've seen us," Bean muttered from the driver's seat. "Be ready!"

Jerking his head up, Rye saw that the gates were being dragged open by a gray-uniformed guard. The wagon chugged on, out of the dimness of the Scour into a sea of light.

"Steady!" Rye heard Bird hiss as the corner of the fence loomed large beside them.

Bean's heavy face did not flicker. His left hand moved over the panel of levers and buttons in front of him. The red pointer on the dial began to crawl backward. The wagon slowed. Bean swung the wheel hard to the right.

Roaring and creaking, the vehicle left the track, trundling between the white marker stones. It rolled through the gateway and stopped with a long hiss of steam.

The gates swung shut behind it. And from his high seat, Rye looked down on the nightmare that was the Diggings.

There were people everywhere — people and their leaping shadows.

Broad pits, their sides studded with tunnels, teemed with laboring figures. The shortest of the slaves hammered and dug in the tunnels, which were all brilliantly lit by some means Rye could not see. Taller slaves hauled buckets of earth and broken rock out of the pits, tipping the spoil into carts drawn by grunting beasts that looked like miniature, hornless bloodhogs. Other slaves hauled at the neck chains of hogs with filled carts, urging them toward a waste pile that towered over a cluster of sagging, flat-roofed huts.

Guards in gray patrolled the pits and the dusty ground above, cracking whips, bellowing commands, lashing out at any slave who fell or stopped work for an instant. Closer to the gate, off-duty guards sprawled around a great bed of glowing coals set on a slab of blackened stone. A huge chunk of meat turned on a spit above the fire, but the guards seemed to have lost interest in it. They were all looking eagerly at the wagon.

"Hoy, trader!" a coarse voice shouted. "You're late!"

The flap beside the driver's seat was pulled aside, and the guard who had opened the gates peered in.

Rye took one look at the brutish face with its flat, cold eyes and felt a creeping horror. For an instant, the urge to cringe back and cross his fingers and his wrists was almost irresistible.

Nothing Bird said had prepared him for this. The man walked and talked like a human. He even looked like a human. But there was nothing human behind those flat gray eyes. The guard was . . . empty. A being without a soul.

Ignoring Bean, the guard stared at Rye, then glanced around the wagon. His jaw dropped as he saw that the storage space was empty except for a few shadowy figures huddled against one wall.

"Where's Four-Eyes?" he demanded. "Where's all the food?"

"The Master needed the trader's wagon to move slaves to a new source of jell," said Rye in the cold, impatient voice Bird had told him to use. "I have picked up some slaves already. The other twenty are to come from here."

"*What?*" the guard exclaimed. "But we can't spare that many! We'll have trouble making this week's jell quota as it is!"

"That cannot be helped!" Rye snapped. He leaned across Bean and thrust the gray paper into the guard's hand. "As you see, you are to supply the twenty mine rats who work in Tunnel 12, and sleep in Hut 16. Fetch them from wherever they are, and be quick about it."

The guard stared blankly at the note, then turned toward the fire.

"Hoy, Krop 1!" he bawled.

A guard who had been sitting at his ease with his back to a withered tree stump stood up with a groan and began walking to the wagon. The first guard went to meet him, holding out the gray paper. As they came back, muttering together, Rye saw with a shock that they were identical. They had the same flat eyes, the same straight, almost lipless mouths, the same smooth, hairless skin that looked as if it would be cold to touch.

The guards both bent their heads over the note, their fingers pressing on the numbers in the last line.

Bird, Chub, Itch, and Bean were absolutely silent, but the tension in the wagon was so thick that Rye felt his head might burst with the strain of it.

"It looks all right, Krop 4," the second guard said grudgingly.

"Of course it is right!" barked Rye. "Are you questioning the Master's orders?"

"No, sir," Krop 1 gabbled. "We were just —"

"Then get the slaves! Make haste!"

The other guards had left the fire now, and were coming to see what was happening. There were eight of them, and a chill ran down Rye's spine as he saw that they all looked exactly the same as the two already at the wagon.

"Bring the mine rats from Tunnel 12," Krop 1 ordered, turning to the approaching group. "They're wanted elsewhere."

After that, there was nothing to do but wait. As the minutes ticked by with agonizing slowness, Krop 1 and Krop 4 stood murmuring together by the wagon. Rye sat stiffly, staring straight ahead, pretending not to listen.

"We'll never make our week's quota now," he heard Krop 1 mutter.

"We wouldn't have anyway," the other guard replied. "This area's finished. Soon it'll only be fit for Scour scum. The tunnels are caving in, and even up here the surface is sinking. It's taking out all the jell that does it. They should leave some of it in the ground."

"We've told them that," said Krop 1. "But they never listen to us. They just —"

Suddenly he started, turned, and thrust his head through the open doorway of the wagon. Rye's heart seemed to leap into his throat.

"The jell scourings, sir!" the guard said, pointing at the metal box. "Did you bring them, at least?"

Rye's face felt frozen as he nodded. Bird had told him the guards would want the trader's jell, but he had forgotten all about it.

He stood up and, awkwardly crouching, felt in the pocket of the stiff coat for the key he had been given. Trying not to fumble, he unlocked the padlock on the metal box and threw open the lid.

Inside was a large pottery crock, tightly corked. Rye struggled to lift it. It was extremely heavy.

"Wait, sir!" shouted Krop 4. "That's a job for mine rats. I'll round some up."

"No!" snapped his companion. "We're losing twenty workers tonight as it is. We can't afford to take any more off the job. You get the jell — I'll bring the replacement jar." He turned and marched briskly away.

His face impassive, Krop 4 moved around to Rye's side of the wagon. One of the figures huddled in the storage space drew a sharp breath — Chub, Rye guessed. The tension in the wagon had risen sharply.

For some reason, Bird and the others were fearful of what the guard was doing.

And suddenly Rye realized why. Suddenly his mind was filled with images of dots and crosses inside a circle, dots and crosses inside a square.

The little patterns on the side of the wagon and on the metal box were messages. They had been put there by the jell-wet fingers of the slaves from Nanny's Pride farm, when it was their turn to unload the trader's jell crock at the Diggings.

And this afternoon, when Four-Eyes's wagon had stopped at the farm, the messages had been seen and understood.

This was how Bird and the others had known which numbers to write into the false orders.

The circle meant "tunnel." The square meant "hut." The dots and crosses were simple sums that disguised the numbers. Three multiplied by two multiplied by two — twelve. *Tunnel 12.* And the sum inside the square equaled sixteen. *Hut 16.*

Krop 4 seized the heavy crock and lifted it with ease. As he stepped back, he caught sight of the little square painted on the side of the jell safe. He squinted at it in dull puzzlement. Rye's stomach fluttered.

Then he heard the thudding sound of hurrying feet. Twisting his neck to look through the front window of the wagon, he saw that Krop 1 was jogging back with an empty crock in his hand. Close behind him were twenty small shambling figures with guards marching beside them.

"Stop dithering!" Rye barked, swinging back to face Krop 4. "My cargo is here at last!"

The guard jumped back just as Krop 1 arrived at his side and jammed the new crock into place. With a snort, Rye slammed the lid, sat down on the box, and pulled the hide curtain back over the doorway.

Bean crouched forward on the driver's seat as the slaves were tossed carelessly into the wagon behind him.

Rye watched, his face a stern mask but his heart wrung with pity, as one by one the stolen workers from Nanny's Pride farm crawled into the dim storage space. They were ragged and exhausted. But none of them showed surprise at seeing Rye or happiness in seeing Bird, Itch, Chub, and Bean. They knew better than to show any emotion at all. They simply crouched together on the hard metal floor as if there was no fight left in them, as if they had no hope.

"Very well!" Rye barked when the last of the slaves was on board. "Open the gates!"

Two guards hurried to do his bidding. Steam billowed upward as the wagon began to ease backward through the gateway.

Rye heard pebbles crack and snap and felt a jolt as the back rollers reached the edge of the track. Bean hauled on the wheel and the massive, chugging vehicle began turning to face the way it had come. The Diggings gates closed.

We have done it! Rye thought, dizzy with relief. *We have —*

He jumped violently, almost falling from his seat, as there was a deafening bang, and the huge white rock beside the wagon's left front roller exploded into dust. Bean yelled in shock, and the wagon came to a shuddering halt.

SLAVE HUNTER

There was a sound like approaching thunder, pebbles sprayed, and a high whinnying split the air. The hide curtain beside Rye was ripped aside, and he found himself staring out at the furious face of a woman on horseback.

Terrified by the hissing vehicle, the horse was plunging and crying out. Pushing a smoking, stubby black tube into her belt, the woman slashed at the animal savagely with a short whip, ordering it to be still, till at last it obeyed, trembling and sweating.

"Didn't you hear me calling, you buffoon?" the woman shouted at Rye. "Get back off the road! There's a cart coming behind me from the Harbor. You'll have to wait till it's passed. Our mission is urgent. We don't want to be stuck behind this lumbering monstrosity all the way through the —"

She broke off, frowning. She peered through the doorway at Bean in the driver's seat, at the small people huddled together in the back of the wagon.

"What's this?" she demanded.

"The Master's business," Rye said, raising his chin.

"No business *I've* heard of," the woman said slowly. "And who, might I ask, are you?"

"Who I am is not your affair," said Rye, putting as much cold pride into his voice as he could. "It is enough for you to know that I am the Master's servant, and my task is of great importance to him."

"Is it, indeed?" the woman murmured. She stood up in the stirrups and looked over the wagon at the guards staring out through the gates.

Rye looked, too, and for the first time read the notice fixed to the mesh.

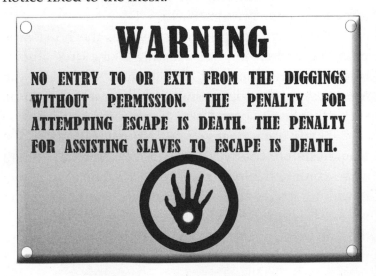

WARNING

NO ENTRY TO OR EXIT FROM THE DIGGINGS WITHOUT PERMISSION. THE PENALTY FOR ATTEMPTING ESCAPE IS DEATH. THE PENALTY FOR ASSISTING SLAVES TO ESCAPE IS DEATH.

"Guards!" the woman shouted. "Why have you allowed these mine rats to leave their work? Explain yourselves!"

The guards glanced at one another in confusion. They muttered together for a moment, then one slipped through the gates and came running. It was Krop 1 or Krop 4, Rye thought, because the gray paper was in his hand.

"We were only obeying orders, Kyte," the guard mumbled, handing the paper to the woman. "We know Brand's sign — seen it often enough."

Kyte! Rye's stomach turned over. "Kyte" was the name on the top of the orders! Kyte was the slave hunter who had led the invasion of Nanny's Pride farm!

The woman glanced at the paper. Her face darkened. "You dolts!" she snarled.

"Get out!" Bird's frantic cry rang out, echoing around the bare walls of the wagon. "Run!"

Bean slammed his hand down on a lever. Steam gushed, hissing, from beneath the wagon, smothering it in a billowing white cloud. As Kyte's horse squealed and reared in terror, knocking the guard beside it to the ground, Bean hurled himself sideways out of the driver's seat, onto the track. Stocky figures bolted out of the storage space and began scrambling after him.

"Run!" screamed Bird. "Bell! Chub! All of you —"

Kyte yelled in fury, fighting to control her panicking mount. The guards behind the gates hesitated, blinded by the steam. Rye leaped off the jell safe and began trying to fight his way through the press of fleeing slaves, toward Sonia.

There was a sharp crack, and a flash of white light lit up the wagon. The flash lasted only an instant, just long enough for Rye to glimpse ragged figures caught in mid-stride, Bird's mouth wide open in a soundless cry, Itch half turned with his knife in his hand, Chub crouched beside a man who seemed to have fallen.

They were all completely motionless. And in the same split second, Rye realized that he, too, had frozen where he stood. He could not move a finger.

It was as if time itself had stopped. But only inside the wagon. Outside, there was noise and activity. Outside, there was shouting, scuffling, cursing, the hissing of steam, the rumbling of approaching wheels, the thudding of fast-running feet. And there was Kyte's voice, high and dominating, rising above everything else.

"Krops, stay where you are! Stay, you fools, and hold the ones you've got! I've quelled the scum in the wagon — and the enemy spy who's leading them, too. The strays can be rounded up later. Good! Here are my Baks with the cart!"

The sounds of wheels and running feet grew louder, slowed, then stopped. Rye tried desperately to turn his head so he could see what was happening on the track, but it was hopeless.

He could only imagine the cart coming to a stop beside the wagon. He could only imagine Kyte looking down from the back of her cowed horse at another set of inhuman gray-clad guards panting between the cart's shafts.

"Take the trench-bridge from the cart, Baks!" he heard Kyte order. "We won't need it now. Then turn the cart around. By chance, we've been spared the journey to the Den. We don't need Scour scum for the Master's test anymore. These traitors will do just as well."

"But, Kyte," whined a Diggings guard as the clatter of falling wood and the sound of turning wheels signaled that the woman's order was being obeyed. "Can't we at least have the mine rats back? We're shorthanded as it is!"

"Silence!" Kyte snapped. "The penalty for trying to escape the Diggings is death. Isn't that so?"

"Yes, Kyte," the guard mumbled.

"Yes!" cried Kyte. "So these scum are doomed to die in any case. And if I were you, Krop, I'd think twice about questioning my orders. You made a bad mistake tonight. If I hadn't come along —"

"It wasn't our fault," the guard protested. "The spy showed the Master's paper, with Brand's signature at the bottom. How did he lay his hands on it?"

There was a tiny pause. Rye knew why. Kyte was well aware that it was her error that had allowed the gray paper to fall into Bird's hands.

"It doesn't matter where the paper came from!" the woman snapped, recovering. "What matters is that somehow the spy knew where the mine rats he wanted worked and which hut they slept in."

"It was not the Krops who told!" exclaimed the guard. "The Krops would never betray —"

"Luckily for you," Kyte cut in smoothly, "I'm in a good mood because I've been spared a tedious journey to the Den. So I'll destroy the paper and say nothing of it to Brand. I'll report that a spy made use of the jell trader's wagon to enter the Diggings and tried to steal the slaves by force."

"Thank you, Kyte. The Krops are in your debt."

The guard sounded very subdued. The woman's reply was coldly triumphant.

"Very well. Forget the paper ever existed, and you'll be safe. And don't open the gates again for any reason till I tell you to do it. Do you understand me?"

"Yes, Kyte."

"Now load the prisoners into the cart. Yours first — the quell will hold mine a bit longer. Tie their wrists and ankles, but don't harm them. They're to be delivered in good condition. The Master wants them to be able to run."

Kyte's final words echoed often in Rye's mind during the long, jolting journey that followed. Bound hand and foot, lying packed together with the other prisoners beneath a canvas cover that hid the sky, he could not forget them. They kept coming back to him like a hideous refrain.

The Master wants them to be able to run. . . .

What horror awaited him at the Harbor?

He had no idea how many others lay with him in the cart. Four-Eyes had been found, released from the sack, and left in the driver's seat of the wagon, still fast asleep. But Bird had been taken, he knew. He had seen her carried out of the storage space with Sonia. Bean was here also. The Diggings guards had grabbed him as he stood helping others to jump down from the wagon. And Itch was here. And Chub and her husband, whose name seemed to be Pepper.

But there were many of the slaves from Tunnel 12 as well — all those who had not managed to escape in those first few moments of confusion. Rye could hear them whispering to one another. Every now and then he would catch a name. Lucky. Giggle. Bud . . .

Lucky, Giggle, Bud, Chub, Bird, Itch, Bean — what sorts of ridiculous names are they? Rye thought with a flash of useless irritation. And slowly it dawned on him that *all* the names of the people he had met since going through the silver Door were strange. Bones. Needle. Cap. Four-Eyes . . .

Then he saw it. Nicknames! They were nothing but nicknames!

The people here believed in the old tale, long forgotten by almost everyone in Weld, that those who know your true name have power over you. They kept their real names secret from everyone but their closest family and friends.

And perhaps this was wise. Perhaps it was their only defense against the sorcerer who had first led them, then enslaved them. Not knowing their names, the Master could control their bodies, but not their minds.

Of course! That was why Rye's careless use of the name FitzFee had caused Bird to react so savagely. Bird's family name must be FitzFee, too. She had thought Rye was trying to enchant her!

If only I had been, Rye thought drearily. *And if only I had succeeded. Then Dirk, Sonia, and I would be together now, facing only the dangers of the Scour. And the bag of powers would still be with me, safe around my neck.*

After a while, he lost all sense of time. And gradually the murmuring of the other prisoners, the bumping of the cart, the pounding of the guards' feet, merged and became parts of confused, nightmarish dreams.

He seemed to see Dirk waking, groggy with myrmon, on the track far behind him. He seemed to see Bones sitting alone by the sled at the Den, his head in his hands.

And he seemed to see Sonia lying somewhere very near, somewhere in the rattling cart, coming to consciousness and searching frantically for some sign of him.

Hazily, knowing he was caught in the web of a waking dream, he sent his thoughts to her.

Sonia, I am here with you! Sonia, we are captured — being carried to the Harbor.

Rye sent the message, as so often he had sent urgent thought messages in the past, without any real hope that it would be received. But this time something was different. Faintly, so faintly that he could not be sure it was real, an answer came to him.

The nine powers. Can you or Dirk reach . . . ?

The stab of pain he felt made him reply abruptly, without thought.

The bag of powers is lost. Dirk, too. Lost.

Sonia's horror rolled like a wave through his mind, making him gasp and blink. Then, quite suddenly, there was another feeling — a feeling, almost, of joy — startled joy!

Rye, we are talking to each other in our minds!

Yes, Rye thought in amazement. But how can that be?

Am I dreaming? He sent the message cautiously.

If you are, then I am, too, the reply shot back, clearer than before. And then another message came, tumbling after the first and tinged with dread. *Rye, I can smell the sea.*

Rye hesitated. And slowly, through the mingled odors of canvas and sweat, he too detected the tangy scent of salt water and seaweed.

He had been relying on his sense of hearing to warn him that the journey was ending. He had been waiting for the dull, regular boom of waves pounding on a shore, like the sound that had dominated the city of Oltan.

There was no sound of waves here. Yet now that he had become aware of it, it seemed to him that the smell of the sea was growing stronger by the moment.

And the cart was slowing. Slowing, turning . . . and stopping.

Rye —

Sonia's voice clamored in his mind, sharp with fear, then broke off abruptly. Rye knew why. Sonia did not want to burden him with her terror.

We will find a way out of this, Sonia. We will survive, as we did in Oltan.

He sent the message as firmly as he could, but the only reply was a faint brush of warmth. Sonia was holding her thoughts back. No doubt she could not stop herself from remembering that it was the Fellan powers that had saved them in Oltan, and the powers were gone.

The canvas above Rye was pulled aside. He lay blinking up at a canopy of weirdly glowing clouds. The smell of the sea rolled over him, driven by a small, sour breeze. The odor was heavier, oilier than the smell of Oltan bay. And there was still no sound of breaking waves — only a soft lapping, and a faint, dull rumbling that seemed to be coming from far away.

Gray-clad arms seized him, and he was lifted from the cart and set roughly on his feet. He found himself standing on a flat, paved space flooded with white light that banished the darkness of the night completely. Directly in front of him was a blank gray wall, so long that he could not see where it began or ended.

Swaying, he looked up, trying to judge the wall's height, trying to see any way it could be climbed. And to his dazed astonishment, he saw a low roof studded with air vents, and pipes from which steam rose.

This was not a wall, but a building — a building with no windows and no doors. A building so vast that it seemed to go on forever.

An iron hand held him upright as the bonds that bound his ankles were cut. All around him, the other captives were being dealt with the same way. Many were staggering and falling to their knees the moment they were no longer supported.

But no one made a sound — not a single gasp or groan escaped anyone, let alone a plea for mercy. Those who managed to remain on their feet helped those who had fallen. And when the cart was empty and Kyte strode forward to confront her prisoners, she found the people of Nanny's Pride farm, recaptured slaves and failed rescuers alike, standing shoulder to shoulder, staring straight ahead, refusing to show their fear.

Rye felt a strong surge of emotion flow into his

mind, mingling with the respect and admiration he was already feeling. He looked across the heads of the silent crowd and met Sonia's shining eyes.

"So the rats are feeling brave," sneered Kyte. "I'll enjoy seeing how brave you are when tomorrow comes, little rats!"

Turning her back on them, she took a slim gray tube from her belt and pointed it at the building. A square section of the gray wall slid noiselessly to one side.

Rye felt sweat break out on his forehead. The opening in the wall shone bright white. Evil streamed from it like water.

"Guards!" shouted Kyte. "Take them in!"

THE HARBOR

The door slid shut behind them, sealing them in. Ahead was a broad passage with walls and floor of dull, smooth gray. White light glared down from the ceiling, but there were no lanterns. There was nothing on the ceiling at all except an occasional small round hole sealed with mesh through which the salty air of the Harbor drifted.

Rye remembered the light that had flooded the narrow stairway as the Warden led him deep into the oldest parts of the Keep. That light, too, had seemed to have no source. But how different it had been! Golden and mysterious, it had lit those steep, winding steps warmly, gently, at one with the magic that had seeped from the ancient stones.

This light was cold — hard and chill as the floor beneath Rye's feet. And the magic he could sense was cold, too. It pressed in on him, touching him with icy fingers, filling him not with awe but with dread.

How could anyone have followed the man who created this? Rye thought. *How could anyone have thought that it was better to trust him than to stand and fight Olt's tyranny? Could they not see what he really was?*

Plainly they could not, Sonia's voice whispered in his mind. *He hid his true nature till he could get them isolated here.*

Rye glanced across the lines of prisoners and saw Sonia almost opposite him. Her shoulders were bowed and she was shambling along with her head down, so that she looked no taller than Chub, who was walking beside her.

Sonia must have felt his shock at seeing her in such despair, because she raised her head a little and looked directly at him. Her eyes were dark with fear, but her message came to him clearly. *So far they have not realized that I am not like the others, and I do not want them to find out. It might be useful. Who knows?*

With Kyte in the lead, and guards on either side of them, the prisoners walked the length of the passage. The silence of the place was like a living thing. Even the guards' heavy boots seemed to make no sound, as if the walls and floor absorbed and swallowed the echo of their tread.

These guards, Kyte's guards, did not look like the Krops of the Diggings. They were burlier, with broad cheeks and pointed chins. But they were just as inhuman. And they all looked exactly alike.

Kyte was nearing what looked like a dead end. A circular design had been painted in the center of the wall.

Rye had never seen anything like it, but its message was clear enough. The candle in the center of the circle had a bar across it, as if it had been deliberately crossed out. Flame was forbidden here.

Without breaking stride, Kyte pointed the gray tube at the sign. A section of the wall slid away, revealing another passage exactly like the first. The door closed the moment the prisoners had moved through it, and the silence seemed to become even more intense.

At last, another smooth wall barred Kyte's way. This time, she halted and adjusted the collar of her coat before raising the gray tube. Then, as a panel slid aside, she swaggered forward, a slight smile on her lips.

She stopped dead as a hissing voice rose from the desk directly in front of the doorway.

"Do you guarantee it, Brand?"

The voice was so filled with menace that Kyte took a step back, and the watchers outside the room shuddered as if blown by a freezing wind.

A man was sitting behind the desk, but he did not seem to be the one who had spoken. He had raised his eyes as Kyte entered the room, but he merely stared at her glassily. His narrow face was gleaming with sweat. His hands were clasped around a black box set in front of him on the shining desktop. His knuckles were white.

He opened his lips with what seemed a great effort. "Yes, Master," he said. "The trial will be successful. I guarantee it. And as for the spies the bird claims to have seen in the Saltings, there has been no sign of them. If they exist, they will be captured very soon, I promise you."

"It had better be so, Brand. I have waited long for this, and I do not tolerate failure."

The hissing voice was coming from the black box. There was no doubt. Rye felt the hair rise on the back of his neck.

"Once, Brand, the people of this island rejected me, and my own brothers united to send me into exile," the voice rasped. "I swore then that I would return. I swore that I would tear out Dorne's heart and use it as even then I suspected it could be used. I swore revenge on the rabble who had raised my doltish elder brother to the high place that should have been mine."

The man gripping the box made no reply. His eyes, still fixed on Kyte, seemed to have sunk more deeply into their sockets. There was a pale line around his lips, and he trembled all over like a man in the grip of a fever as the low, venomous voice whispered on.

"How fitting it is that both my brothers are dead while I live on in greatness! How fitting that they quarreled, and the younger was forced to flee, as he had forced me to flee! How fitting, Brand, that he — *he* — began the great work that will make me invincible! And how fitting that the rabble who rejected me at last turned against Olt as well, and in their ignorance opened the way for my return!"

The horror Rye felt at that moment was like nothing he had ever felt before. It was as if the ground had fallen away beneath his feet. It was all he could do to remain upright.

This evil being whispering from the black box was not Olt's younger brother. This was the other — the sorcerer who in his exile from Dorne had become the terrible Lord of Shadows.

And Dorne was open to him because of Olt's death, the death Rye had caused.

Rye had been warned. He had heard Olt's claim that only his power kept Dorne safe from its ancient enemy. He had heard the fears that enemy warships were lurking offshore in the east, in the hope that Olt would die.

But he had not believed it. So Olt's long life had ended, the charm had been broken, and the enemy had swooped, destroying the tyrant of the east, taking over all he had built.

And it would not stop there. Perhaps at this very moment, enemy warships were sailing into Oltan bay. And FitzFee and his family, the brave fisherman Hass, all the other innocent, hardworking people who had rejoiced at the death of Olt, would wake to find themselves enslaved again — this time by a being whose evil knew no bounds and who could never be defeated.

Rye was swaying where he stood. Sonia's horrified dismay was clamoring in his mind, but so great was his own shock that he could not even try to make out what she was saying.

"Who is speaking?" the voice hissed sharply. "Who is with you, Brand?"

Horrified, Rye realized that his thoughts, and Sonia's, had been detected. He struggled to make his mind a blank.

"No one is speaking, Master!" gasped the man behind the desk. "And no one is with me — no one of importance. It — it is only . . ." He swallowed, unable to continue.

"It's only Slave Hunter Kyte, Master," Kyte said, stepping forward eagerly. She was afraid, Rye could feel it, but she was not going to miss this chance to impress the Master.

"I've brought the specimens for the test tomorrow, Master," Kyte hurried on. "And, Master, I'm happy to tell you that among them is —"

"Kyte!" the voice broke in coldly. "You were the one whose task it was to find the laboratory workers I sent to help prepare for the test. According to Brand, you brought back only one of the six. I found this . . . disappointing."

Kyte stiffened but defended herself without any outward sign of panic.

"Perhaps Controller Brand didn't tell you the full story, Master," she said, with a spiteful glance at the man sitting at the desk. "Your servants' ship missed the Harbor entrance and fell foul of the rocks. I found bodies washed up on shore — those that the sea serpents hadn't taken. But I also saw footprints leading away from the water and knew that one man had survived. I tracked him and didn't rest till I'd found him."

If she had been expecting praise for her cleverness, she was disappointed.

"Fortunately, the rest were not needed, it seems," the voice replied indifferently. "The test will be held on time. That is all that matters."

And despite all he knew, Rye's blood ran cold at the utter callousness of a being who could take so lightly the deaths of five laboratory workers and the whole crew of a ship.

You are not in Weld now, Rye. . . .

"So, Brand!" the voice of the Master hissed. "You will keep me fully informed as the test progresses. If it succeeds, I will come to Dorne and you will be rewarded. If it does not . . . you will regret it."

There was no further sound or sign, but suddenly it was clear that the evil presence that had been dominating the room had vanished.

Brand's hands slipped from the black box. His hollow eyes regained a spark of life. He straightened his shoulders and glared at Kyte.

His hair, slicked straight back from his bony forehead, was thin and peppered with gray. His narrow face was closely shaved. The high collar of the plain black robe he wore gaped slightly around his scrawny neck.

Once, lulled by the placid security of Weld, Rye would not have feared such an ordinary-looking man, but now he knew better than to be deceived by appearances. He recognized Brand as a cold and calculating enemy. He could see that Brand had no more feeling for others than the desk at which he sat, or the master he served. Brand cared for no one but himself, and would stop at nothing to get what he wanted.

"You take too much upon yourself, Kyte!" Brand snapped at the woman standing in front of his desk. "How dare you barge in here uninvited, pushing yourself before the Master!"

"I didn't know you'd be speaking with the Master, Controller Brand," Kyte drawled insolently. "And I didn't know that you found your conferences with him so . . . disturbing. I came to tell you —"

"Whatever it is, I do not wish to hear it!" Brand snapped. "Get out! Cage the specimens! And if you tell anyone what you have heard here, you will be sorry! Do you understand?"

"Perfectly, sir," Kyte spat. She spun around and marched out of the office.

As Brand's door slid shut behind her, she turned to face the right-hand wall of the passage.

"We'll go this way, I think," she said, glancing over her shoulder at her prisoners. "I'd like you to see what you can expect tomorrow."

She lifted her gray tube. A gap opened silently in the wall's blank surface, revealing a bare little room no bigger than a storeroom. Smiling very slightly, Kyte waited as the prisoners were herded into the room, then she strode in after them and turned her back to face the door.

The door slid shut. The lights dimmed. Packed together so tightly that they were unable to move, the prisoners waited in silence. There was a tiny creak, then a strange, breathy sound, and suddenly it felt to Rye that the room — the room itself — was sinking into the earth!

Someone gave a tiny moan, quickly cut off. A guard sniggered.

Then, as suddenly as it had begun, the sense of movement stopped. A shaft of scarlet light lit the dimness, broadening as the door of the room began to slide open once more.

A strong, unpleasant odor drifted through the gap. Rye recoiled.

"J-jell!" he heard Itch mutter. "And smoke."

"Mixed with something else," Bird whispered back. "What is it?"

Death, thought Rye.

And at the same moment, he realized that Sonia was sharing the horrific picture that had formed in his mind. He had not meant to send it to her — he had not even been thinking about her — but she had received it all the same.

Her reaction shook him to his core. There was fear in it, certainly. But there was elation, too. Then her voice came to him.

We did it! We have found them!

There was no need to answer, for already they were being herded out of the little room, into the red light. The smell was very strong. Figures in gray coats and black gloves were turning to look at them, some with what looked like weapons in their hands. And all around them huge skimmers flapped and lunged, their pale, ratlike snouts smeared with blood, their needle teeth bared, the spurs on their hind legs raking the air.

The prisoners cringed and cried out in terror. Kyte laughed.

"Oh, the slays can't touch you now," she jeered, patting the air in front of the nearest skimmers to display the invisible barrier that confined them. "They're caged by the Master's sorcery. But tomorrow morning it'll be a different story — for you, at least, little rats!"

Already the gray-coated figures had gone back to their work. Kyte swaggered up to one of them and tapped him familiarly on the shoulder.

"So, Vrett, we meet again," she crowed. "I was just talking to the Master about you — telling him that you were none the worse for your ducking in the sea. I've brought the specimens for the test. Do you want to see them?"

The man turned. It was Sholto.

THE CELL

Rye gave a choking cry. He lurched forward, bumping into Bird, who was in front of him, his mind empty of everything but the fact that Sholto was alive — alive!

It did not matter what Bones had said. It did not matter that Four-Eyes had the Weld lantern. Sholto was here, in the red place, as he had been in the dream, his hair clipped brutally short, his lean face gaunt but alert. . . .

Sonia's frightened thoughts flew to him like arrows. *Rye, no! It cannot be —*

With a growl, a guard caught Rye by the neck and jerked him off his feet.

"Do not damage him!" Kyte ordered shrilly. "Put him down!"

"He tried to attack you!" the guard protested, lifting Rye higher and shaking him like a cloth doll.

Pinpricks of light began to explode before Rye's eyes. All around him people were shouting and skimmers were shrieking, their pale wings beating at the invisible walls of their cages.

"Let him be!" shouted Bird. Furiously she threw herself at the guard. He slapped her away as if she were an annoying insect, sending her crashing to the floor.

Then suddenly he doubled up as if he had been punched in the stomach. His eyes bulged with shock. His hand opened, and he let Rye drop.

Gasping, Rye fell to his knees. He could hear the other prisoners crying out. He could hear the guard who had seized him making choking, gobbling sounds. He could hear Chub crying to Bird, dragging her to her feet, and the other guards barking at the remaining prisoners.

Then silence fell abruptly. Feet paced toward him. He raised his head.

Sholto was looking down at him with distaste and without a trace of recognition. Beside him was a severe-looking elderly woman with thick eyeglasses. She was dressed like all the other workers in the room, but the badge clipped to the collar of her gray coat read "Supervisor." She was glaring at Kyte.

"How dare you disrupt our work, Slave Hunter?" she snapped. "These slays are being fed, and it is a delicate task. You had no business bringing the specimens through here — particularly if your guards are incapable of controlling them."

"I thought you'd want to examine them," Kyte said sulkily.

"Of course! But in the right place and at the right time."

Sholto had been regarding the prisoners with cool interest. "I understood that goats were to be used for the test," he drawled.

Kyte laughed. "Goats were used for the early trials. But this time, the goats have two legs instead of four. The Master wants the test to be as realistic as possible, now that the work's nearly completed. Don't tell me you're squeamish, Vrett?"

Sholto raised an eyebrow in such a familiar way that Rye's breath caught in his throat.

"Save your humor for your guards, Slave Hunter!" snapped the supervisor. "They may appreciate it. We do not."

She gestured irritably at the prisoners, her frown deepening. "And what are these stunted creatures? I thought you were to bring full-sized specimens from the Scour."

"These mine rats are marked for death, so I judged it more efficient to bring them instead," Kyte replied carelessly. "Scour scum can be used next time."

She nudged Rye with the toe of her boot. "And this one is full-sized, Supervisor — perhaps your disability has prevented you from noticing that."

The supervisor adjusted her eyeglasses angrily. "I can see it perfectly well! But he is only one of —"

"He's an enemy spy, as it happens," Kyte went on, her offhand tone barely concealing her triumph. "Controller Brand wasn't interested in the fact that I'd captured him, but I'm sure the Master will feel differently."

The supervisor started. She bent and peered at Rye, and when she straightened, her manner had become less aggressive.

"Indeed," she said, bowing very slightly to Kyte. "Controller Brand will be . . . corrected. The Master will be very pleased to hear that the spy has been caught. And he will be most interested to know how the slays deal with him."

She turned to Sholto, who had drawn out a small notebook and begun taking notes. "You can examine the specimens fully when they have been fed and watered, Vrett. They will be in better condition then. Pay particular attention to the spy. I only hope he has not been injured by that fall." She stared coldly at the guard who had dropped Rye.

The guard's shoulders were hunched, and he was still clutching his stomach.

"The tick kicked me!" he complained.

"What if he did?" Kyte retorted. "Are you getting soft, that you can be upset by a little tap?"

"Stand up," Sholto said to Rye.

Rye did as he was told. His thoughts were in turmoil. Was Sholto only pretending not to recognize him? Playing a part in order to deceive Kyte and the supervisor?

Or was Sholto's mind no longer his own? Did he really believe he was Vrett, loyal servant of the Master? The journal fragments showed only too clearly that he had been suffering from delusions. The sorcery of the Harbor might well have completed what the Saltings had begun.

Either way, Rye knew he must not again risk exposing his brother by the slightest word or sign. If Sholto was acting, Sholto would somehow let him know. Hoping against hope, he stood like a statue as his brother's thin, gloved hands ran impersonally over his body. But there was no whisper in his ear, no change of expression on the pale, intent face so close to his own.

"He is well enough," Sholto said, stepping back.

The supervisor turned to Kyte. "You may go, then," she said coldly. "But I trust you will see to it that there is no noise whatever in the next room. I do not want the breeding slays too much disturbed. Your passing will excite them enough as it is. Vrett? Let them out!"

Sholto drew out a gray tube and aimed it at the room's far wall. A door slid open, releasing a flood of white light. The supervisor turned away, raising one shoulder as if to screen Kyte even more completely from her sight.

Kyte winked slyly at Sholto. "Would you like to join me for breakfast in my apartment after the test, Vrett?" she murmured. "The food I can offer is better than the slops you get in your staff feeding room — and certainly the company will be far more enjoyable." She laughed scornfully, glancing at the supervisor's rigid back.

Sholto's face relaxed into a half smile. He bowed slightly.

Very pleased with herself, Kyte turned and led the way to the doorway. And it was not until Rye had shuffled after her with the other prisoners — not until he was actually moving through the gap into the next room, and facing another terrifying array of skimmers — that he realized something was wrong.

There was no shadowy red glow here. The only signs of red were the thick pads of jell that lined the bottom of every skimmer cage. The only shadows were inside the tiny round air vents that dotted the ceiling. The room was large, white, and bright with light. But the skimmers were flapping and clawing just as savagely as the skimmers in the first room had done. The light did not seem to trouble them at all.

And their eyes . . . their eyes were not white, like the eyes of the dead skimmer Rye had seen in Tallus the healer's workroom. They were colored.

Some had a brown tinge, but most were a murky gray. All the eyes were fixed avidly on the passing prisoners, and all glittered with ravenous hunger as jaws gaped and ragged wings beat uselessly on invisible bars.

And suddenly Rye was back in the waiting room of the Keep, listening to Tallus talking excitedly to the Warden.

Skimmers hunt at night because they cannot *hunt during the day!* Tallus had said. *Because daylight renders them helpless! It is their one weakness.*

Not these skimmers, thought Rye. And his mouth went dry as he realized what was being done here, deep in the Harbor building. The Master was raising new generations of skimmers — skimmers that could live in light, attack in light!

Perhaps there were only a few of this new breed now — possibly this room held them all. But in time, the numbers would increase to hundreds, to thousands!

Then they would be sent to Weld. And trapped inside their Wall, under attack that never ceased by night or by day, the people would be unable to do anything but huddle in their homes till the end came.

It would not take very long.

Mindful of the supervisor's warning, Kyte was hurrying them through the room. Rye tried reaching out to Sonia in his mind but he received no answer. He looked for her and saw her in the middle of the group of prisoners, not far behind him.

She was between Itch's sisters, two dark, pretty girls who looked very alike. She was dragging her feet as if every step was an effort. Perhaps she had not even noticed the light or the eyes of the skimmers.

Or perhaps she *had* noticed, and the horror had snuffed out the last spark of her fiery spirit. Of all the things that had happened on this dreadful night, Rye found that thought the hardest to bear. It seemed the end of everything.

Blindly he shuffled along with the other prisoners, paying no attention to his surroundings. Doors opened and closed. Everywhere the stench of skimmers mixed with the duller, earthier scent he now knew was jell.

Finally, at the end of a long passageway, the ropes binding his wrists were cut, and he was pushed with the other captives into a dim gray cell containing nothing but a pile of thin mattresses, a bucket of water, and a heap of bread. One of the round air vents was set in the ceiling, but like all the others, it was covered by metal mesh and was no bigger than Rye's fist.

Kyte raised her gray tube. There was the familiar sound of a door sliding into place, but this time, the door could not be seen. Only a slight shimmer across the doorway showed that the cell was sealed.

Kyte grinned through the invisible barrier. "Make the most of your last night, scum," she jeered. "I'm going to a meal far better than bread and water, and a well-earned rest. But never fear. I'll be attending the slay test in the morning. I wouldn't miss it for the world!"

Then she was gone, and the guffawing guards were gone also. And Rye and the other prisoners were left alone to try with all their might to break through the doorway and to find there was no hope. The invisible seal was as strong as iron.

"Surely Witch could shatter the magic," panted Chub, wiping her forehead. She made for Sonia, who was huddled in the shadows of the back wall of the cell.

"She is not a witch!" Rye exclaimed furiously. "How many times do I have to tell you? Leave her be! She can do nothing to help us!"

"Then our only hope is to overpower the one called Vrett when he comes to examine us," said Bird, scooping water from the bucket and splashing her hot cheeks.

"He won't come into the cell," Pepper said in a low, trembling voice. "He's a cold, careful creature — you can see it in his face. He'll stand outside and make notes in his cursed little book."

"Then we'll trick him — *force* him to come in!" Bird spun around to Rye, water still dripping from her hands. "They're more interested in you than in any of us, Spy. If you pretended to be sick or in pain . . ."

Bean grunted agreement. "He told that sour supervisor you weren't badly hurt, Spy. It'd be on his head if you died. And it's a wonder you're on your feet, that's a fact. That guard could've broken your neck."

"At least he g-got a kick in the b-belly for his trouble," Itch put in.

There were a few snorts of laughter. Rye said nothing. He could not remember kicking the guard. It seemed to him that all he had done was dangle helplessly, being shaken till his teeth rattled.

"So is it agreed, Spy?" Bird snapped. "You'll play your part?"

Rye swallowed and nodded. The plan was a good one — even better than Bird realized, for she did not know about the concealing hood hidden under the black coat. Now that his wrists were free, he could pull the hood over his head. Everyone could join hands, and with luck, he would be able to lead them all, invisible, to safety. The thought of luring Sholto into a trap made him feel hollow inside, but he knew he had no choice. He had to face it. Sholto was the enemy now.

"Witch *is* sick, I think," Chub called in fright from the back of the cell. "Sick or in a trance! I can't wake her!"

Rye's stomach turned over. The little crowd parted for him silently as he hurried to Sonia's side.

Sonia was lying very still. Her eyes were closed. Rye knelt beside her and took her hand. He murmured her name. She did not stir.

Sonia! he called to her in his mind. *Sonia, wake! Please wake!*

The girl's eyelids fluttered. Slowly her eyes opened. Seeing Rye, she yawned, pulled herself up into a sitting position and blinked around, shivering.

"Cold . . ." she mumbled.

She had only been very deeply asleep, it seemed. Filled with relief, Rye pulled off his coat. As he wrapped it around Sonia, a tiny roll of paper slid from one of the pockets and dropped onto the floor.

Rye had checked the pockets of the coat when he had first put it on, and they had been empty. Since then, he had added nothing except the hoji nuts he had been feeding to Snaffle the clink. Puzzled, he picked up the paper and unrolled it.

* Legs straight.
* Arms well muscled.
* Tense.
* Eyes clear.
* Red hair.

"What is it?" Sonia asked faintly.

"A — a page torn from Sholto's notebook," Rye stammered, squinting at the paper in the dim light. "Notes on what I look like. I saw him taking them. But how it came to be in my pocket I cannot —"

Then suddenly he remembered Sholto patting him all over, checking for breaks and strains.

He looked again at the brief notes. Then he saw it. And his heart swelled till it seemed that it would burst in his chest.

"Read the first letter of each line," he whispered, thrusting the paper into Sonia's hand.

Sonia looked at the paper. "L-A-T-E-R," she read slowly. Her eyes widened, and suddenly she shook herself, as if to banish the last effects of her exhausted sleep.

There was the soft sound of a door opening and closing. Measured footsteps began pacing along the hallway, toward the cell.

"He's coming!" Bird hissed from the doorway. "For pity's sake, Spy, lie down! We won't get another chance at this!"

"Hoy, you! Vrett!" Itch bellowed. "C-come quickly! The spy's sick! We think he's d-dying!"

The footsteps broke into a run. Bird and the others shrank back to the sides of the cell as Sholto appeared in the glimmering doorway, his eyes searching frantically for Rye.

Rye stood up. Ignoring the shocked and furious cries of the other prisoners, he ran to his brother.

"Sholto!" he gasped, pressing his hands to the invisible barrier. "We thought you were dead!"

Sholto shook his head. "Rye, what are you doing here?" he said furiously. "By the Wall, you have ruined everything!"

PLANS

It was not at all the greeting Rye had expected. As he stared at Sholto, aghast, he suddenly realized that he no longer had to look up to meet his brother's eyes. He had grown taller since Sholto went away, and now they were almost the same height. Once this would have pleased him enormously. Now it merely added to his feeling of strangeness.

The other prisoners were whispering, their voices hissing behind him like foam on the shore. They had not attacked him, as he had half expected. Perhaps Sonia had defended him by quickly explaining why he had not tricked Sholto as he had promised.

"W-we came to find you, Sholto," Rye stammered. "Dirk and I thought —"

"Dirk?" Sholto snapped. "Dirk is *alive*? But where is he?"

"He was left in the Scour," said Rye. "He was . . ."

A great, aching lump rose in his throat. It was impossible to explain — impossible to find the words, with Sholto's angry eyes upon him.

You have ruined everything. . . .

Rye understood only too well. Sholto had made a plan. Working alone and in constant danger of discovery, he had been gathering the information he needed to carry the plan out. And now . . .

He heard Sonia's footsteps behind him. She took his arm, and he felt her loyalty to him and her fury with his brother flow through him in equal measure.

"Sholto, are you going to stand there snarling at Rye, or are you going to free us?" she demanded.

Sholto raised his eyebrows. Sonia's appearance had plainly taken him by surprise. Like Kyte and everyone else, he had thought she was one of Bird's people. Now that she was standing upright, with Rye's black coat draped around her shoulders, he could see his error.

Typically, however, he made no comment and asked no questions. He merely answered her. "I cannot free you," he said in a level voice. "I am sorry."

The blow was so great that Rye staggered where he stood.

"Are you saying," Bird shouted as her companions cried out in dismay and disbelief, "that you'd rather watch your own brother being eaten alive than risk giving yourself away? What sort of man are you?"

Sholto's lips twisted wryly. "A man who should

have made his meaning clearer, it seems. I can release you from this cell, but I cannot free you. Brand is taking no risks of spies interfering with the test. I heard just now that this floor has been cut off from ground level. Brand has taken the lifting chambers under his own control. Our door wands will not operate them. We are all trapped down here."

He frowned down at the slim gray tube in his hand. "And even if we were not," he went on doggedly, "there would still be no escape. The whole Harbor building has been sealed and will remain sealed until after the test tomorrow. No one can get in. And no one can get out."

A heavy silence fell. Sholto went on, his voice very calm. Only Rye could have had any idea of the misery he was feeling.

"Guards will be patrolling this floor for the rest of the night. If they find this cell empty, they will search until they find you — and find you they will, make no mistake. They will smell you out wherever you are hiding."

"We know that as well as you do, Spy's Brother," Bean retorted before Rye could say a word about the concealing hood. "But I'd rather die fighting guards than stay in here waiting to be slaughtered by those — those monsters you are helping to breed."

His companions murmured fervent agreement.

"We can do better than die fighting guards," Sonia said quietly.

Rye looked at her. So did everyone else.

Sonia's eyes were very green. She shrugged. "If we have to die in any case, why not take the monsters with us?"

"And how would you propose doing that?" Sholto drawled.

"Set this place on fire and burn them," said Sonia, meeting his cool gaze defiantly. "Burn them all!"

Yes! Rye's heart gave a great thud.

Sholto's face was like a pale mask. He leaned forward. "If fire was remotely possible, I would have used it by now. Do you imagine I would have let the skimmers live and breed one moment longer than I could help?"

Sonia stared at him, a puzzled crease deepening between her brows.

"There is no fire at the Harbor," Sholto said. "Did you not see the signs? Flame — or anything capable of making flame — is forbidden."

He leaned closer, and now everyone in the cell could see and recognize the frustration that had made deep grooves in his pallid skin and hollowed his dark eyes.

"Heat and light are created here by some means I have not been able to discover," he said. "None of the substances kept here will explode, alone or mixed together —"

"What about that?" Bird interrupted, pointing to the weapon at Sholto's hip.

Sholto shook his head. "It blows smoke, that is all. Smoke calms the skimmers a little so they can be fed, just as it calms bees when honey is to be taken from a hive. But somehow the smoke is created without fire by —"

"Sorcery," Chub hissed.

Sholto looked down his nose. "By some means I have not yet been able to discover," he finished severely. "The point is, there is no way to burn this place."

A sigh gusted around the cell. Sonia looked devastated. She turned away, pulling the stiff black coat more closely around her shoulders.

Rye's eyes had not left his brother's face. "Fire may not be possible," he murmured. "But you have thought of another way of destroying the skimmers, Sholto, I know you have. What is it?"

"There is no point in discussing it," Sholto said impatiently. "It is just an idea, and now I will never have the chance to try it. I am new here, and some are still wary of me. Once it is known that you have escaped from the cell, I will be the first to be suspected of helping you. Even if they cannot prove it, they will watch my every move from now on. Still . . ." He shrugged. "Whatever comes of it, I cannot leave you here."

He raised the opening wand and pointed it at the shimmering barrier in front of him. As it whispered and slid aside, he stood back. Plainly he was expecting the prisoners to rush the doorway.

But no one moved.

"You call the monsters 'skimmers,' Spy," Bird said, looking at Rye. "They are known, then, where you come from."

It was not a question, but a statement.

Rye met her earnest eyes. Again, she reminded him strongly of FitzFee. He knew it was time for the truth — at least as much of the truth as he was free to tell.

"The Master has been sending them to attack us," he said simply. "That is why we came here — to try to stop him."

"And we came between you and your goal," Bird said soberly. She exchanged glances with Bean, Itch, Chub, and the other prisoners. They seemed to come to some silent agreement.

"Well, you and Witch had better go about your business and help your brother carry out his plan," she said briskly. "We'll stay here in the cage. With luck, the guards won't realize that anything's amiss. Then at least we'll go to our deaths knowing that something good will come of this."

Sholto gaped at her, his calm mask slipping for once. "That is — truly noble," he muttered after a moment. "But I fear your sacrifice would be pointless. The guards will notice that Rye is missing. They will be looking out for him in particular. He is the enemy spy — Kyte's prize! And the supervisor knows about him, too."

He shook his head in sudden, furious impatience. "Besides, I have no plan worthy of the name. I have an idea, certainly, but I have no way of carrying it out. I do not know enough yet. I need more time —"

"There is no more time," Rye said, suddenly knowing it was true. "The daylight skimmers are ready — we heard Brand tell the Master so! And if the test is successful, the Master himself will come here. He will see you, Sholto! He will know you are not the real Vrett! Our only chance is to —"

He broke off and looked up. He could have sworn that he had heard a tiny chittering sound, coming from somewhere above him.

All he could see was the small, dark disc of the air vent in the ceiling. The chittering sound came again. Then there was a little thud and a furious scrabbling sound. The wire mesh masking the vent bent, quivered, bulged, and abruptly burst open. And Sonia screamed in shock as a small, chattering streak shot from the open vent like an arrow and plunged deep into the pocket of the black coat hanging around her shoulders.

"By Nanny's b-beard!" gasped Itch. "A clink!"

Sonia had thrown off the coat in panic. It lay in a heap on the floor, heaving slightly. Crunching noises were coming from the pocket.

"It is Four-Eyes's clink!" Rye exclaimed. "I cannot believe it! She followed me all the way here just to get the last of the hoji nuts!"

"Sshh!" hissed Sonia. "Listen!"

Rye froze. So did everyone else. And in the silence they heard a low, ghostly whisper drifting from the air vent.

"Rye! Rye, are you there?"

Rye's heart leaped.

"Dirk!" Sholto gasped, his drawn face suddenly alive.

Rye moved hurriedly to just below the air vent and looked up. "Dirk!" he called softly. "Where are you?"

A gasp of relief sounded through the vent. "On the roof," Dirk's voice whispered. "Bones found a rope. The clink led me straight to this air vent."

Bones? thought Rye in amazement. Then he shook his head. This was no time for idle questions.

"I cannot see a way of getting you out," Dirk whispered. "The cursed place is sealed tight. I had been hoping to find an answer on the roof, but there are no trapdoors and the air vents are no bigger than my hand. I will keep looking. But in the meantime, Rye — here!"

There was a soft, sliding noise, and the little brown bag of powers dropped from the open vent into Rye's outstretched hands.

A ripple of sound ran around the cell as Sonia caught her breath and Bird's people shrank back, crossing their fingers and their wrists.

"The hood," Dirk was whispering from above. "Do you still —?"

"Yes," Rye managed to say, touching the silken folds on the back of his neck. "I have it."

He became aware that Sholto had come into the cell and was standing beside him, but he could not tear his eyes from the bag. He could hardly believe it had returned to him. With trembling fingers, he tied the frayed ends of the broken cord together and pulled the knot tight.

"Bones found it lying beside the track," Dirk said. "It is a miracle he saw it. I pray it will help. Rye, is Sonia with you?"

"Yes," Rye said. "And Sholto."

"*Sholto!*"

"Greetings, brother!" Sholto drawled. "It seems that neither of us is dead, despite all reports to the contrary."

He grinned broadly as a stream of astounded curses hissed from the air vent. But the grin quickly faded.

"Dirk, listen!" he said rapidly. "There is something you must do. It is vital, brother! Are you listening?"

"Yes," said Dirk cautiously.

"You cannot help us, I promise you. Leave here now! Find your way home, as quickly as you can. Tell the people to abandon the city — break through the Wall and get out."

"Break through the *Wall*? Sholto, are you —?"

"Listen to me! If the Warden tries to stand in your way, rouse the people to rebel against him. You can do it, if anyone can. Tallus will help you. People close to the Keep could use the Doors to escape, if the Warden can be made to see reason."

"But —"

"Dirk, the skimmers are being bred to attack in daylight as well as by night. And they are being bred to fly in the cold of winter, as well as in the summer heat. The time is coming when nothing will stop them — nothing!"

"It is true, Dirk," Rye burst out. "The new skimmers are here. I have seen them!"

"Outside the Wall, the people will have some chance of survival, especially if you are leading them," Sholto went on, his voice very cold. "If they stay inside it, they will have none. Do you understand?"

There was dead silence. Then:

"I understand," Dirk said, his grim voice echoing hollowly down the narrow shaft.

Sholto closed his eyes briefly, and everyone in the cell could see some of the tension that had held him rigid draining away.

"Go, then!" he murmured. "Go in safety. Tell our mother that Rye and I . . ."

He could not finish. He pressed his thin lips together and looked down.

"I will tell her," Dirk said softly. "Sholto, I have listened to you, now *you* listen to *me*. Trust Rye. Much has changed since you saw him last. He can help you more than you know."

With that, he was gone.

Rye stood motionless, desolate, gripping the little brown bag. Sonia slipped her arm through his. "You had better go, too, Rye," she urged. "You and Sholto."

"And you, Witch," Chub urged.

But Sonia shook her head. She bent, picked up the coat still lying on the ground, and slipped it on, ignoring the chittering of the clink in the pocket.

"Give me your cap, Rye," she ordered.

Rye pulled the dark cap from his head and silently handed it over. Sonia pulled off the orphan's helmet and jammed on the cap in its place.

"There," she said, buttoning the coat up to her throat. "Now if I lie down and pretend to sleep, the guards will think I am you. We are almost the same height, and they have never seen me standing upright."

Rye met her determined eyes. He swallowed the lump in his throat. "Whatever happens, we will be together at the end," he said evenly. "We will be back as soon as we have done what we have to do."

Sholto was looking stunned — almost afraid. "This is madness!" he muttered. "You are all putting too much faith in me."

"We are putting our faith in Spy and his magic," said Bird, and Sholto stared at her in startled confusion.

"I hear boots," Bean growled. "Guards . . ."

There was no more time for argument.

In moments, Sholto and Rye were outside the cell, Sholto had sealed the door, and Bird and her people were lying huddled together with Sonia, pretending to be asleep.

But now they could all hear the tramping feet, very near.

Sholto looked around quickly. "Hide in those shadows, Rye," he hissed, pointing to a dark corner beside the cell. "Stay very still. I will try to turn their attention in the other direction."

Rye pulled open the neck of the brown bag. He put on the horsehair ring and slid the armor shell onto the tip of his little finger.

Sholto looked down his nose. "By the Wall, Rye, what is this? Surely you do not believe that charms will —"

"Take my arm," Rye said, and pulled the hood over his head.

THE DISPATCH AREA

Sholto's jaw dropped as his brother vanished before his eyes. Speechless with shock, he made no protest as Rye dragged him out of the path of the approaching guards, whispering to him not to make a sound. But perhaps it was only when the guards had tramped by them without a glance that Sholto realized he was as invisible as Rye, for he looked down at his own hand with such a comical expression that Rye almost laughed.

"How is this possible?" Sholto breathed, when the guards were well past. "How does a simple piece of fabric baffle the eye? It must be something to do with the way it reflects the light! By the Wall, Rye, where did you —?"

"It is a long story," Rye whispered back. "I know you will not believe me if I tell you the hood is magic, Sholto. You do not have to believe it. Just accept that it works. Now, tell me your plan for destroying the skimmers."

"I am going to show you," Sholto said grimly. "Plainly that is the only way to convince you that there *is* no plan." He led Rye farther down the passage to a place where a far shorter, darker passage branched off to the right.

A few steps along the second passage, Rye found himself facing a red wall bearing a large black-and-white sign.

EXTREME DANGER!
DISPATCH AREA

Sholto raised his door wand. The red wall slid away. Behind it was a tiny room, even smaller than the lifting chamber. Strange black garments hung from hooks on the room's side walls. The wall ahead was blank. *Another door*, thought Rye. He was sure he knew what was beyond it. He swallowed, trying to quell the fluttering in his stomach as the red panel whispered shut behind him.

Sholto took two of the black garments down, passed one to Rye, and began climbing into the other. The garments were rather like the climbing suit Dirk wore for work on the Wall of Weld, except that they were complete with hood, gloves, and pockets for the feet. The black fabric was very light and slippery, and the front opening had no buttons but sealed at a touch.

"Do we really need these?" muttered Rye. "I am still wearing the hood."

And the armor shell, he added in his mind. But he had decided not to mention the power of the shell until he had to. It was something Sholto could not explain away, and he had been shaken enough by the hood.

Sholto turned his head. Encased in dull black, he looked like a frightening stranger. Even his face was covered. Only his eyes were visible, peering through a transparent screen.

"This fabric has its own 'magic,' " he said dryly, his voice only slightly muffled by his hood. "It seals in human warmth and scent. The new skimmers do not only hunt by sight, remember, little brother."

The fluttering in Rye's stomach grew worse. He finished putting on his own overalls and waited in silence as Sholto opened the inner door.

The space beyond the dressing room was warm, dim, and so vast that Rye could not see where it ended. The straw that covered the floor was clotted with dried blood and droppings. And the low ceiling, strung with sturdy wires, was thick with skimmers — line after line of skimmers hanging upside down like huge pods on a vine.

The beasts' ragged wings were folded. Their eyes were closed. They were as large, or larger, than the dead skimmer Rye had seen in Tallus the healer's workroom. Now and again, one stirred, disturbing its neighbors, and there was a small burst of irritated flapping and quarreling before the creatures settled to sleep again.

"Can these skimmers also fly in daylight?" Rye breathed.

"They can survive it, but most cannot hunt prey quite as well by day as by night," Sholto whispered back. "Their young are a different story. You saw them in the cages on the way to the cell. It is an amazing improvement in just one generation — all thanks to jell in large quantities, of course."

"Jell?"

"Jell is the key. We had no idea, Rye! We thought jell had no really useful purpose. But it does. It helps plants and animals adapt to different conditions very quickly. The more jell is present, the faster a species can adapt. No one seems to know why, but it is so."

Sholto sounded fascinated. He *was* fascinated — Rye could see it in his face. Sholto was truly appalled by the danger of the new breed of skimmers, yet he could not help being interested in the process that had created it.

Rye wet his lips. "So if skimmers are exposed to light, and there is a lot of jell in their cages, their young will cope with light better than they do," he murmured haltingly. "And the *next* generation will cope better still."

Sholto nodded. "I have not been able to find out how long the breeding program has been going on. I am supposed to know all about it already, so have to be careful what questions I ask. But I do know that the skimmers in the workrooms are regarded as the final product. The best — or worst — of them will be used in the morning's test."

The eagerness faded from his face. His somber gaze met Rye's, and abruptly an image of the captives they had left behind in the cell rose between them. Rye shivered. Sholto pressed his lips together and turned away.

"What I wanted to show you is at the far end," he said. "Follow me. Be as quiet as you can."

Rye did not need the warning. Even with the armor shell firmly in place, it was terrifying to creep below the pale, heavy bodies of the sleeping skimmers, to see the pointed snouts and the needle teeth hanging just above his head. The creatures seemed to snarl even in sleep. If one should lose its grip and fall . . .

The walk seemed endless. By the time they reached the far end of the enormous room, Rye was soaking with sweat.

"There," Sholto whispered.

He was pointing to something on the back wall. It was a large, dark gray circle that began at the height of Rye's waist and stretched up almost to the ceiling.

The circle was edged with what looked like a tight roll of dark fabric. Rye reached out and touched the dark edging. It was smooth and soft, like bread dough. It sank a little when he gingerly pressed it, and bounced back when he took his finger away.

"I think this circle is a door," Sholto said. "And I think the black rim shows that a pipe or tunnel can be attached to the outside of the doorway before the door is opened. That black material makes a very tight seal. The same means is used in the workrooms, when skimmers need to be moved from cage to cage — though there, of course, the doors and pipes are much smaller."

"A tunnel!" Rye caught his breath. "Sholto! That must be how the skimmers are sent to Weld!"

Sholto frowned and rubbed his forehead. "That was my first idea. This room is called the 'Dispatch Area,' after all. That seems to mean that skimmers here are to be dispatched — sent — somewhere else. But I have never seen this door open, and I know these skimmers are hand-fed. It is a mystery."

"Perhaps there is another vault for the skimmers that go to Weld," Rye whispered eagerly.

"If there is, I have not found it," Sholto said. "And Kyte says all the beasts are kept on this level."

Perhaps in his frustration, he had spoken too loudly, for a skimmer near to them suddenly grunted and stretched its wings. Its neighbors lunged at it irritably, shrieking and flapping. Rye and Sholto froze, flattened against the wall, as slowly the beasts settled once more.

"Enough of this!" Sholto muttered. "We must get out of here. Rye — if you insist on knowing my secret weapon, put your ear to the wall."

Wondering, Rye did as he was told. And to his astonishment, he heard the lapping of water. He could even feel the vibration of swirling movement against his cheek and with the palms of his hands. He turned back to his brother, his eyes full of questions.

"The sea is on the other side of that wall," Sholto said. "For some reason, this place was built so far down on the shore that when the tide rises, much of the back wall of this floor is below the level of the water."

He stood on his toes and reached up till his fingertips almost touched the top of the circle. "The tide comes at least to here," he said. "I have felt it."

Rye felt heat rush into his face. "So if we could get the door open . . ."

Sholto nodded. "If we could get the door open at high tide, the sea would rush in with huge force. I have calculated that it would take an hour at most to flood the whole lower floor of this cursed place and drown everything in it. My plan was to disable the lifting chambers first, so none of the new skimmers could be saved."

He smiled grimly. "Skimmers drown quickly," he added. "I learned this in Weld. I designed a water trap for Tallus, just before I left, to help him catch specimens for examination. I often wonder if it worked."

"It worked very well," Rye murmured. He was thinking that it was typical of Sholto not even to mention that the flooding of the building would have meant his own death as well. Even if he had survived the first raging torrent bursting through the round doorway, he would have drowned afterward, with everyone and everything else.

Sholto had clearly considered this and decided the sacrifice was worth it. But he would not want Rye to speak of that.

Keeping his face to the wall, Rye felt for the light crystal inside the little brown bag. He drew the crystal out, smothering its light with his hand, sheltering it from the skimmers with his body. He heard Sholto gasp but did not stop to explain. Quickly he pressed the crystal to the center of the door.

A window appeared in the dull gray circle, but there was nothing to be seen — just thick, swirling darkness. Then something long and pale floated across the darkness. Rye squinted, trying to make out what it was, and suddenly realized it was a trailing frond of seaweed. This part of the door was underwater!

He pushed the crystal higher. And now he could see the oily, sluggishly heaving surface of the sea, and several gray ships, each with a round black circle marked low on its side. In the distance, there was a line of white foam.

"What is that foam?" he asked.

"It must mark what they call the breakwater," Sholto said, his voice trembling slightly as he gaped at the crystal in his brother's hand. "The breakwater was built across the mouth of the Harbor to hold back the waves and make the water safer for ships at anchor. Rye, that device is . . ."

His voice trailed off as he saw that Rye was not listening. Rye had looked above the breakwater, above the open, foam-flecked sea beyond. He was staring at the sky — at the massed gray clouds edged with brilliant red that boiled on the horizon. His face was filled with dread.

"I had lost track of time," Sholto said heavily. "I had not realized dawn was so near."

"That is not the dawn," Rye whispered, and he began to shiver all over.

The red-rimmed clouds were not normal clouds. Evil was within them — an evil so powerful that it turned his blood to ice. He had felt something of it when he first entered the Harbor building. He had felt it since. But now he knew that what he had felt was simply a trace, an echo, a shadow. Nothing had prepared him for this.

He became aware that Sholto was tugging at his arm, whispering urgently. With a great effort, he pulled the crystal from the wall, closed his hand on it to dim its light, and pushed it back into the little bag. Dizziness almost overcame him. He swayed and felt his brother's wiry arm wrap around him.

"Oh, Rye, I am sorry!" he heard Sholto murmur in a broken voice that sounded nothing like his own. "Fool that I am! I should not have allowed myself to be persuaded . . . I should not have allowed you to hope. Dirk would have known better. He is good with people — I am not. But that is no excuse. . . ."

Rye took a deep breath, willing himself to stop trembling, willing the dizziness to pass. Sholto had seen nothing in the red-rimmed clouds but the first signs of daybreak. He thought Rye's dread had been an attack of panic for the prisoners in the cell, for himself, for Weld, because time was running out. There was no point in trying to explain.

"Come, we will go back to the cell," Sholto was saying softly, trying to pull him away from the wall. "At least we can release the captives and give them a fighting chance."

Rye shook his head. "The tide is rising," he croaked. "We must open this door."

Sholto's worried expression abruptly changed to a glare of baffled fury. "We cannot open it, Rye! Can you not get that through your thick head? I do not have the power to open it. For all I know, there is not a person in this whole accursed place who has! And nothing will break the seal. Even skimmer venom does no more than dull the surface. I have tried it! I have tried everything!"

Rye clenched his fists and stood his ground. "There must be a way. There must! We have to stop —"

"Rye, what has come over you!" Sholto hissed. "You used to have sense! Have the tricks in that wretched bag turned your brain? Have you begun to think that just because you wish for something it will be so?"

"They are more than tricks," Rye hissed back, closing his hands protectively around the little brown bag. "They are *magic*, Sholto!"

"Indeed!" Sholto jeered, hardly troubling to keep his voice down. "Then if you have magic at your command, why can *you* not open the door? Wizards in fairy tales can always get through locked doors. The sorcerer Dann was famous for it, I am told."

The bag warmed beneath Rye's fingers. And suddenly he remembered the golden key.

He felt in the bag and pulled out the tiny key. Then he thought again. He dipped his fingers back into the bag and drew out something else as well.

"What is this?" Sholto demanded, his eyes on the key.

"I am not sure," Rye replied calmly, turning to the wall. "I have been waiting to find a lock this key will fit, but perhaps I did not understand it. We will see. Hold my arm tightly, Sholto. Just in case."

He reached up and touched the key to the center of the dark gray circle that Sholto thought was a door. He twisted his wrist.

There was a faint clicking sound. The gray circle slid away. And with a roar, the sea burst into the room.

TRAPPED

Rye had not really believed it would happen. It had been an idea — the glimmer of an idea. But suddenly he and Sholto were off their feet, tumbling beneath a cold, salty, battering torrent, clinging together by a miracle.

Dimly, Rye heard Sonia crying out in his mind. No doubt she had felt his sudden stab of shock and fear. But the fear had passed almost instantly. Now he was exultant. With savage joy, he felt the sea serpent scale he had taken from the bag of powers sink deep into the flesh of his hand. He felt serpent strength flow through him. He felt his body become one with the flood.

He gripped his brother tightly. He surged with his brother up to the air. He flung himself forward and rode the wave created by that first massive explosion of water till at last it cast them down by the sealed entrance at the other end of the vast room.

And then, clinging together knee-deep in water thick with sodden, stinking straw, Rye and Sholto looked back. And they gaped in awe as the sea gushed through the huge gap the golden key had opened, and the water rose, and the skimmers died.

For the skimmers, woken, shrieking, flapping, fighting one another for space to fly, were attacking the noisy, swirling flood. They did not fear it, because they did not recognize it for what it was. To them, sound and movement meant only prey. Muddy eyes on fire with a ravenous hunger that was never satisfied, they plunged, snarling, to their deaths. They clawed at tumbling clumps of bloody straw, sank their needle teeth into writhing strands of seaweed, slashed at long-dead fish and rolling bones. Then they went under, their wings flailing helplessly as the rushing water dragged them down.

The air was thick with them. The dark water gushing through the wall was swirling with them. In moments, the eddying lake that the floor of the huge room had become was filling with pale bodies struggling and dying.

And still the sea poured in, and still the water rose, and still the skimmers attacked, till the flapping and shrieking had ended, and there was no sound except the ceaseless roaring of the flood.

"We must open — the doors!" Sholto gasped, ripping off his black head covering. "The water must reach the workrooms — the daylight skimmers. None must survive to breed!" He was numb with shock, but he knew what he wanted. He wanted the sea to take possession of every corner of the cursed building that was the skimmers' breeding ground. He wanted the sea to sweep away every skimmer in existence, to flood the nest, to drown it.

"The cell first," Rye said. "Then the rest."

For it had come to him that the key could save them all. It could save Sonia, and Bird's people, and it could save him and Sholto as well. It could free them from the Harbor. It could give them a chance to escape the horror in those swollen, red-rimmed clouds.

Sholto's door wand, soaked through, was dead and useless, but the entrance door slid open at a touch of the golden key. Water surged into the dressing room, and the door did not close again. The hanging black garments floated and tangled in the rising tide as the brothers waded waist-deep to the outer door and opened it as well.

And then there was nothing to stop the sea. It surged through the short passage and spilled into the larger corridor. Straw, weed, and dead skimmers floated with it, bobbing and swirling. Rye and Sholto splashed through the debris, turned to the left and began to run.

"There!" cried Sholto, pointing as they ran. "There, Rye, there!"

And for all his eagerness to reach the cell, whenever Sholto called and pointed, Rye reached out and touched a place on the wall with the golden key. Then he would see a door slide open, and water spill into the room beyond.

Every moment, he expected to see gray-coated figures dart, startled, from the gaping doorways. Every moment, he feared the sight of guards pounding along the streaming passage.

But no one appeared. Rye's heart began to sink.

By the time he and Sholto reached the cell, he knew what he would find. He knew what he would find, but he looked anyway, hoping against hope.

As he had feared, the cell was empty.

This was why they had seen no guards. This was why no one had come to investigate as doors opened and water flooded into the workrooms.

The underground floor was deserted. The prisoners had been taken, and everyone else had gone to witness the test.

"We are too late," he said bleakly.

Without a word, Sholto turned and ran. Rye did not call after him. He knew where his brother was going. He knew what he would say when he came back.

Too late.

Rye closed his eyes. He was remembering the cry of fear that had come to him when the sea first gushed through the wall. He had thought Sonia was feeling his panic, but it had been the other way around. He had been feeling hers. That had been the moment when the guards came for the prisoners sooner, far sooner, than any of them had expected.

Too late. The terrible words were clanging in his brain, on and on, like the tolling of a great bell.

Like the bell of Oltan summoning the people on Midsummer Eve, Rye thought. And into his mind drifted the memory of Hass the fisherman's dark, anxious face, and Hass's earnest voice begging him to be still, to keep hidden, to accept that he was powerless to stop what was going to happen.

It's begun, Hass had said. *The bell is tolling. Nothing will stop it now.*

But I did stop it, Rye thought. *I stopped it. And I can stop this.*

He heard splashing behind him and turned around. Sholto was plodding back, his head down. When at last he reached Rye and looked up, his face was sagging with despair.

"The workrooms are flooding. The bases of the cages are dissolving in the salt water, as I had hoped. The skimmers there will die. But the skimmers chosen for the test have gone. They are safe. I cannot believe it. We came so close . . ."

"It is not over," Rye said. His voice sounded harsh and strange, even to himself. "Where is the testing room?"

Sholto shook his head. "On the upper level of the building somewhere, but where, I have no idea."

"Show me the nearest way to the upper level!" Rye begged. "Show me, Sholto!"

Sholto stared at him. Then, without a word, he turned and led the way past the deserted cell. He pointed to the wall. A door slid open at a touch of the golden key, but behind it, there was only dark, echoing space.

"There is usually a lifting chamber here, but the guards would have used it to take the prisoners and the skimmers up to the test," Sholto said as water rushed past them into the dark space. "No doubt it waits at ground level, blocking the shaft, and I have no means of calling it down. Its twin on the other side of the workrooms is certainly in the same state. The supervisor and the others from the workrooms would have gone that way."

He took a breath. "So we are stranded down here," he went on in a level voice, his eyes on Rye. "The water is rising quickly — even more quickly than I had hoped. All that remains for us is to escape the building through the gap in the Dispatch Area wall. Better to drown quickly, under the sky, than slowly between these cursed walls."

We would not drown, Sholto, Rye thought, touching the smoothness of the serpent scale with a fingertip. The scale was beginning to loosen, but it would soon sink into his palm again when it felt water.

And for a moment, he imagined bearing Sholto through the oily swell of the Harbor, dragging him to shore, and hurrying with him back to the Saltings. The speed ring would aid them. The hood would hide them. The armor shell would protect them. In no time, they would catch up with Dirk. Then they could all, all three of them, find their way back to Weld.

Leaving Sonia to be torn to pieces without lifting a finger to help her. Leaving Bird and her people to suffer the same fate. And leaving the worst of the daylight skimmers alive, to breed at the Master's evil will.

No. Rye thrust the idea of flight aside, hating himself for even allowing it to cross his mind. But what if he and Sholto escaped into the sea and then circled back and tried to get into the building by one of the outer doors?

No. That would take too long — far too long. He could feel it in his bones.

"We must find another way to the upper floor," he said aloud.

Sholto shook his head. "There is no other way. Believe me, Rye. I have searched this level from end to end. I have found and mapped every door. I have entered every room except . . ."

Rye pounced. "Except what?"

"Except the room where the guards sleep," Sholto replied reluctantly. "My door wand would not open it. The guards' area is strictly forbidden — that was one of the first things I was told when I came here. But I am certain there is no way out from there. The guards use the lifting chambers like everyone else."

"Where is the door?" Rye said urgently. "Where, Sholto?"

Sholto looked down pointedly at the water eddying around his knees. Then he sighed as if he no longer cared what he did, and led the way farther along the passage till they reached a sign on the wall.

Rye put the golden key to the sign, and a door began sliding open.

The stench that rolled out of the widening gap was so vile that he jerked back, his hand pressed to his nose and mouth.

Then his heart thudded as he realized that something was driving the smell. There was a draft — a draft of cool, sea-smelling air. And there was light!

Water was already pouring through the doorway. Rye felt it tugging him on as he stumbled forward, dragging Sholto with him. And the door, like all the other doors they had opened, did not close behind them.

Rye had the impression of enormous, echoing space, but for a moment, all he could do was stare straight ahead. The wall facing the door was in two sections, one set above the other. The bottom half, as tall as the wall of a normal room, was made of dark, oozing stone. It was like the walls in the dungeons beneath Olt's fortress. Plainly it marked the end of the underground part of the building.

The top half of the wall was the usual gray. Smooth and sheer, it stretched up toward a flat roof so high that it made Rye's head spin. But it did not quite reach the roof. It stopped short, leaving a gap screened by black iron bars. The light of early morning was flooding through the bars, as if the space on the other side was open to the sky.

And Sonia was there, in the light. Rye could feel it as surely as he could feel the draft blowing softly on his face, and water swirling around his knees. He took a step forward, heard Sholto make a muffled sound, and only then turned and saw what loomed close by him, to his left.

It was a giant cage made of thick iron mesh. It almost filled the vast room's floor space and rose to just below the roof. And perched high inside it were two monstrous winged beasts.

His eyes still dazzled by the light, Rye thought at first that the creatures must be the dragons of legend. Then he made out feathers, spines, and vast curved beaks, recognized the evil reek of ash and rotting meat, and realized what he was seeing.

This cage, two stories high in the heart of the Harbor, was the roost of the Master's creatures — the giant birds Bones called "sky serpents."

Rye half smiled. So the terror that had attacked him at the very beginning of this ill-fated quest was to confront him at the end. Well, so be it.

"Why in Weld are you smiling, Rye?" Sholto whispered, sounding as close to panic as Rye had ever known him to sound. "Come out of here — now! There is nothing beyond that wall of stone but earth and sand. It is part of the foundations of the building! And the guards sleep here, with those stinking birds! By the Wall, how do they bear it?"

"They are not human," Rye said, glancing at the beds of straw, the tubs of drinking water, and the gnawed bones that lay around the base of the cage. Already the water surging through the open doorway was turning the floor of the room into a swamp.

Sholto gritted his teeth. "What does it matter what they are? Rye, come away! Do you not see? There is no way forward from here."

Rye looked up, narrowing his eyes at the glare coming through the barred gap below the roof.

"There is," he said. "Those bars are far enough apart for us to be able to squeeze between them, I am sure of it."

There was no reply. Rye glanced around and what he saw in his brother's face made him realize that Sholto thought he had taken leave of his senses.

"This room is two stories high, Sholto," he went on, forcing himself to speak calmly, though his heart was racing. "Part of the upper floor is on the other side of the gray section of the wall. It is the place where the test is to be held. Sonia is there, and the other captives. We must get to them before it is too late."

"Are you mad?" Sholto cried, his control breaking at last. "You cannot know what is on the other side of that wall, Rye! And even if what you say is true, we cannot get through those bars! We cannot reach them!"

The giant birds in the cage cocked their heads. Perhaps they had heard Sholto's voice only as a faint cheeping far below, but they had heard it. They squatted on their perches, very still, listening.

"We can," said Rye.

He slipped the golden key into his pocket and opened his clenched fist. The armor shell still bulged on the tip of his little finger like a huge deformed fingernail. But the serpent scale was lying loose and glimmering in the palm of his hand. Only an oval-shaped red scar remained to show where it had buried itself into his flesh.

"What is that?" Sholto hissed, looking down in horror at his brother's outspread hand. "What is that scar? And what is that — that *thing* on your little finger? It looks like —"

Rye pushed the scale back into the brown bag that dangled around his neck. When he drew his fingers out again, he was holding the small red feather. As Sholto stared at him wildly, he shrugged.

241

"There is no time to explain," he said. "The iron of the cage will slow us, and it will make us faintly visible as well, but we have to take the risk."

He held out his scarred hand. And Sholto, his face expressionless, took it, and allowed himself to be led to the stone wall.

Rye edged into the corner of the room — as far from the sky serpents' cage as he could get. He lifted his arms. *Up!* he thought.

And slowly, falteringly, the magic of the feather drew him and Sholto up the sour-smelling stone wall, up past the smooth gray wall above, and onto the ledge where the bars began. And then the monstrous birds saw them and came swooping and screeching, battering their wings on the iron mesh of the cage.

THE TESTING HALL

The light pouring through the bars was dazzling. The great birds were gigantic shadows, lunging and shrieking at the intruders they could see only as ghostly outlines. Their eyes streaming, Rye and Sholto clung to the bars and peered through to the room on the other side.

The first thing they saw was bright sky. Vivid squares of clear blue sparkled above the silvery grating that stretched over the testing hall. Sunshine streamed through the grating, and now that he was so high, Rye could feel its warmth.

He thought of Dirk, and in his mind, Dirk's face was framed in that bright, sunny blue. But no doubt wherever Dirk was by now a sullen pall of gray cloud still hung over the tortured earth. No doubt the blue was just a solitary patch over the Harbor building, and the Master would allow it to gleam only for as long as the test continued.

The monster birds screeched in fury. Again and again their talons rasped on the mesh of the cage, setting Rye's teeth on edge. He felt Sholto's fingers tighten painfully on his arm, and looked around.

Sholto's face was gray and gleaming with sweat.

"I — daresay this gap was left to give the birds more air," he said, his lips barely moving. "It — is very convenient for us. But I wish it was not — so far above the ground." He swallowed.

Rye cursed himself. How could he have forgotten? How could he not have realized what this climb had cost Sholto? Sholto was amazingly agile and had lightning reflexes. He could dodge a danger or duck into hiding faster than anyone Rye knew. But he had always feared heights. That was why it had been understood in the family that he would never be able to follow in his father's footsteps and become a Wall worker, like Dirk.

As a schoolboy, Dirk had taken mischievous delight in climbing onto the roof of the house in Southwall and walking close to the edge, just to make Sholto turn pale and sick at the sight while young Rye laughed.

"Come down, Dirk!" their mother would scold, if she caught him. "What would the Warden say if he saw you playing such dangerous games? And do not think you are better than Sholto because you can climb without fear either! Sholto is good at other things."

But not the things that mattered to Dirk, or to me, or to our father, in those days, thought Rye. And for the first time he realized that Sholto, for all his learning, might have had all his life the sense of not being good enough — a feeling that only his mother had suspected.

At this moment, Sholto was no doubt thinking that Rye would have done far better if he had had Dirk as a companion in this desperate adventure.

Wondering guiltily if this was why thoughts of Dirk kept floating into his mind, Rye pressed closer to the bars and looked down.

The room beyond the bars was very large — more like a meeting hall than an ordinary room. Long balconies jutted from all four walls. Slight shimmers in the air showed that invisible barriers shielded them. The balcony on the wall Rye was facing was the only one that did not have a narrow staircase leading up to it from below. The front of its transparent shield bore three large black circles.

"Almost certainly the skimmers will be released through those openings," Sholto said, jerking his head slightly at the circles and clearly making an enormous effort to keep his voice even.

Rye nodded, relieved that the balcony was still deserted.

The balcony below the bars was also empty. The other two, on the shorter walls to Rye's left and right, were filled with seated men and women wearing black uniforms or gray coats. Some of these were looking at the balcony with the circles, eager for something to happen. Most were looking down.

"I am going to try to get through the bars," Rye hissed in Sholto's ear. "Then you can follow. Do not worry, I will not let you go."

He waited for his brother's sick-looking nod and then turned sideways and pushed his way between the bars. It was a tight fit, but by wriggling a little, he managed it. Sholto slid through easily, but his face, when he was finally standing beside Rye with his back to the bars, was the color of goat cheese.

Rye looked down, and, despite the heat of the sun pouring through the grating above, his forehead was suddenly beaded with cold sweat.

The prisoners were directly below him, hemmed in by guards. Kyte the slave hunter was strutting up and down in front of them, high black boots shining, belt bristling with weapons, making the most of her moment of glory.

Her guards stood facing her, shoulder to shoulder. Their backs formed a solid gray barrier across the corner of the testing room, pressing their captives into a huddle.

Rye made out Bird and Bean, standing side by side. There was Itch, his arms around his sisters. There were Chub and Pepper, hand in hand. There were all the other prisoners from Nanny's Pride farm. And there, behind them all, her back to the wall, was Sonia.

Rye's chest tightened painfully. In her severe black coat and cap, Sonia seemed to tower over her companions. Her head was bowed so her face was hidden from view, but other than that, she was standing very upright, making herself look as tall as possible. Despite the terror that must have been clutching at her heart, she was still pretending to be Rye.

Sonia, I am here, just above you, Rye called to her in his mind. *I am trying to think what it is best to do.*

He thought he saw Sonia give a tiny start, but she did not raise her head.

Just do not think too long. . . . The answer floated into his mind, light as a falling leaf.

"Is there anything in your bag of tricks that you can use as a weapon, Rye?" Sholto asked.

He was still as pale as wax, but he too was looking down — down at the prisoners, and at the guards surrounding them.

"No," said Rye. "But if I can reach Sonia and the others — close enough to touch them — I can protect them, at least."

And what then? he wondered, but could think of no answer.

Sholto raised his eyebrows. "Then we had better get down there, brother," he said softly, looking up and meeting Rye's eyes. He nodded across the room.

There was movement behind the screen of the balcony with the three black circles. Controller Brand, clutching the black box, was standing to one side with the gray-faced supervisor. They were both watching as guards pushed three huge transparent cages forward. Each cage was alive with flapping, snarling skimmers.

Rye's mind went blank. Behind him, the giant birds shrieked. Below him, the people in the balconies were stirring with excitement. But all he could see were the skimmers, with their ragged wings, their rat-shaped snouts, and their mud-colored eyes, being wheeled closer and closer to the edge of the sunlit balcony, closer to the three circles.

Then he distinctly heard a crack, a clang, and a muffled curse, directly above him. He jerked his head up and to his utter astonishment saw Dirk scowling down through the grating, blue sky brilliant behind his head.

For a moment, Rye froze. For an instant, he thought he must be dreaming. Then he saw Dirk pull the broken skimmer hook free from the corner of the grating, which was bent and partly lifted, and he knew that what he was seeing was real.

Dirk had not left the Harbor. He had never left the roof! He had been here all along, trying to pry the grating over the testing room open, using the shrieks of the monster birds to disguise the sound.

"The cursed thing has snapped!" Dirk muttered to someone beside him, throwing the hook aside.

"Dirk!" Rye called softly.

Dirk jumped and looked wildly around.

"Here!" Rye said, between the screeches of the birds. "Just below you. I am wearing the hood. Sholto is with me."

"Dirk, for Weld's sake, why are you still here?" hissed Sholto. "Did I not tell you —?"

"How could I go when I saw blue sky appear above this part of the building and heard the iron of the roof slide open?" Dirk retorted, pressing his face against the grating and squinting down in an effort to see them. "By the Wall, it is more than even you could expect of me, Sholto! But I cannot get through this cursed grating! Rye, where is Sonia?"

"Down below, with the others," Rye said. A great, aching lump rose in his throat.

Then his heart gave a jolt as a familiar hollow-eyed face appeared beside Dirk's, wild spikes of white hair shining in the sun.

"The lady?" cried Bones, blinking rapidly and frantically clicking his beads. "The lady's in danger? I hear sky serpents a-roaring and a-screeching! Is that —?"

"No!" Rye managed to say, refusing even to think about how Bones and Dirk happened to be here, and together. "The birds are caged, in the room next to this one. But, Dirk, the Master's people are going to release skimmers in here! The new skimmers that can see in daylight! We have to get Sonia and the others out! But they are surrounded by guards. . . ."

"Yes, I see them," Dirk said grimly, blinking down through the grating. "Here, give me that, Bones!"

Silently the old man passed him a long, heavy white bone that looked like one of the precious bloodhog bones from the sled. Dirk stuck the end of the bone into the gap made by the bent corner of grating and pushed upward till the sweat stood out on his brow.

Nothing happened. The square of grating did not budge.

"The key, Rye!" Sholto muttered. "Try the key!"

Rye looked up at the twisted, upturned corner of grating. Sholto was right. What was that broken grating but a kind of door?

He dug the tiny key from his pocket, stood on the tips of his toes, and reached up, straining higher and higher till the key touched the bent corner. And without any sound at all, the square of grating folded neatly back, leaving a man-sized hole.

Bones whooped and clapped his hands to his cheeks in amazement. But instantly, without an exclamation or a question, Dirk was slipping through the opening, sliding down the nearest bar one-handed, and swinging himself into position beside Rye and Sholto. He gripped Rye's shoulder to gain the protection of the cloak, but he did not need the feather to hold him steady — no one who had been a worker on the Wall of Weld would have needed that.

"Bones!" he hissed, holding up his hand. "The rope!"

A length of thick rope slithered down through the hole in the grating. Dirk grabbed the end and held it, gathering the slack over his shoulder.

"It is tied to an air vent and is secure," he said crisply. "Now! Our best plan is to lift Sonia and the others to safety. Even invisible and armored, we cannot hope to get them out on the ground, past so many guards. Agreed?"

He waited for his brothers' nods before going on.

"Sholto, you go up onto the roof. It is almost flat. You will feel safer there. Bones will haul you up. Rye, put the feather away. We will get to the ground much faster without it. You and I will slide down the rope and —"

"No!" Rye barely recognized his own voice. As his brothers gaped at him, he cleared his throat.

"It will be better if I go down alone. I do not know how strong the feather's power is — how many people it can raise at one time. On the ground, you will add weight, Dirk, but if you stay up here you can lower me down and also pull on the rope when the time comes, to lift us more quickly."

"He is right," said Sholto at once.

Dirk hesitated for a split second, then nodded.

Tucking the feather into his pocket with the key, Rye took the rope Dirk thrust at him and grasped it firmly, about a body length from the end. He saw by his brothers' faces that the rope had almost vanished from sight when he touched it. Good. That was what he had hoped. Once he was away from the iron bars, the hood should hide him and the rope completely.

There was a strange ringing in his ears. Everything seemed unreal, but his mind was very clear. He looked down at Sonia's bent head.

Sonia, we can escape through the roof. I am coming down to you with a rope. It will not be visible, but everyone must be ready to take hold of it the moment I land. And everyone must be linked.

Sonia's answer came in a flash.

We will be ready.

No doubt she had not intended it, but a gale of other thoughts and feelings came on the heels of those simple words. Rye felt them, and his heart swelled.

Sonia knew that the plan was desperate. She realized that if it were to have any chance of success the prisoners would have to be off the ground, out of reach, before their captors realized they had vanished. But she wanted to live. She wanted them all to live. And she was determined that Rye's effort would not be in vain.

"I think you will be visible when I am gone, even holding the rope, because you will have no direct contact with me," Rye said rapidly to Dirk and Sholto.

"And the others will be visible, too, once they reach you and break contact with the hood. I will have to come up last, to keep the feather and the armor shell working till the end. But with luck no one will look up here — they have other things to interest them."

He glanced across the hall to the balcony on the other side. The guards had gone. Figures in gray coats were fixing large clear pieces of pipe to the black circles on the skimmers' cages. Other figures were attaching the free ends of the pipes to the circles on the balcony shield. Brand was sitting down, the black box on his knees. The supervisor was still standing, watching her workers intently.

"Wish me luck," Rye said.

He felt Dirk and Sholto grip his shoulders briefly before letting him go. Then he stepped into space.

THE ROPE

irk fed out the rope slowly and steadily, so that it seemed to Rye that the drop to the floor of the testing hall took forever. In fact, it was only seconds before he was landing, gently and without a sound, beside Sonia.

He knew that Dirk had felt the tension on the rope slacken, because the next moment, a few coils of spare rope slithered to the floor behind him. He gathered them up quickly and looked around.

Sonia had prepared her companions well. They had all drawn a little away from the guards and turned to face her. Their arms were linked. Not one of them jumped or cried out as an invisible presence landed among them. The chance of rescue had overcome their dread of magic, it seemed.

"Here!" Rye whispered, holding out the coils of rope. "Make haste!"

And in seconds, Bird's people were reaching for the lifeline they could feel but could not see. They did it in the order they had plainly decided beforehand. Itch and his sisters first, Chub and Pepper next . . .

Rye glanced at Sonia standing tensely beside him. They could both hear Kyte's booted feet striking the paved floor, but the guards blocked their view of her. Above their heads, the monster birds shrieked and tore at the mesh of their cage.

"Listen to those stupid beasts!" Rye heard Kyte complain. "Their noise is unbearable — and they're right above our viewing balcony, too!"

Rye held his breath, praying she would not look up. If she did, she would soon see the reason for the giant birds' fury. She would see Dirk and Sholto standing motionless in their high corner perch, while the birds' razor-sharp talons raked the mesh of the cage on the other side of the bars.

"The birds are hungry, Kyte," mumbled one of the guards. "You should have let us release them to hunt before we brought the prisoners up. The Master wouldn't like it if he knew —"

"If the Master's pets are hungry, it is not my fault, but Brand's!" Kyte broke in. "*Brand* was the one who broke into my rest, ordering me to move the prisoners long before they were needed."

And at that moment, Rye realized that, more quickly than he had thought possible, the people of Nanny's Pride farm were all gripping the rope and all touching one another. Bird and Bean were the last. They were panting as if they had been running, but their faces were set, and their eyes were gleaming with determination.

Rye pulled the red feather from his pocket. He put his arm around Sonia, and together they formed the last links in the human chain.

Now, Rye knew, the hood concealed them all. Anyone watching from above would have seen the whole group of prisoners vanish. Urgently he tugged on the rope.

Up! he thought, as much to Dirk and Sholto as to the Fellan magic he had come to trust. *Up!*

And with joy he felt his feet leave the floor. He felt himself rising steadily. He felt Sonia's relief and heard the high, nervous chattering of the clink hidden in her pocket. He looked up and saw Bird, Bean, and the others clinging to the rope like grapes on a stem, and Dirk and Sholto pulling together high above, their faces anxious and sweating.

Then he looked down. He was well above the heads of the guards now, almost to the level of the balconies, and the guards had noticed nothing. They stood like figures carved of gray stone, listening to Kyte, watching Kyte swaggering up and down before them, little knowing that behind their backs there was nothing but a patch of bare, paved floor.

We are out of their reach, Rye thought gleefully. *Way out of their reach. They cannot touch us now.*

Kyte was still talking. Her voice floated up from below, sneering and confident. Rye wondered grimly how confident she would feel when she found her prisoners gone.

"... nothing but foolish nerves and fuss!" Kyte was saying. "The test could not begin till full daylight, after all — but that is typical of Brand."

"We could have opened the roof of the cage room and let the birds out first," a guard mumbled. "It wouldn't have taken —"

"Brand said 'at once' so I obeyed him to the letter!" Kyte barked. "Perhaps next time he will listen to me! Or perhaps there will not *be* a next time for Brand. Perhaps the Master will decide that he is not fit —"

"KYTE! THE SPECIMENS ARE GONE!" Brand's roar, made terrifyingly loud by some means Rye could not begin to understand, burst like an echoing thunderclap through the great room.

The shock was frightful. Rye heard a strangled cry from above as someone jumped violently. The rope twisted and swung, almost slipping from his hands. Clinging on for dear life, he caught a glimpse of Brand. The Controller was standing up, shouting, his swollen face pressed to the balcony shield, the black box in his hands, his eyes bulging as he stared down at the place where the prisoners had been.

"WHERE ARE THEY? KYTE, YOU FOOL ..."

Do not think about him! Sonia whispered urgently in Rye's mind. *Do not think of anything but —*

Chub's despairing cry rang in Rye's ears. His head jerked up, and above him he saw disaster.

Chub was clinging to the rope with one hand. Her other hand was straining toward Pepper — straining down, uselessly, because Pepper was falling, his arms flailing as he tried to save himself.

Rye knew what had happened as clearly as if he had seen it with his own eyes. The human chain had broken. Shocked and terrified by the sudden roar of Brand's voice, Pepper had lost his grip on the rope, and on Chub's hand. Chub had done her best to hold him but had not been able to bear his weight. He had slipped from her grasp.

And now Pepper was sliding jerkily through the desperately clutching fingers of the people below him. Pepper was falling down and down as the rope swung wildly, Brand roared, and the guards milled around, shouting in astonishment because their prisoners had vanished. Moaning in shame and terror, Pepper was crashing into Bird, who caught him but could not stop him. Pepper was snatching at Sonia, succeeding only in tearing off the black cap so that her coppery hair fell about her shoulders. And then Pepper was sliding helplessly over Rye and, making a last frantic effort, grabbing Rye's shoulder with one hand and with the other pulling the silken hood back from Rye's head.

The watchers in the balconies leaped to their feet, gaping and pointing at the prisoners who had suddenly appeared in midair. There was nothing cold and calm about them now. No sound came through their safety screens, but Rye could see their mouths moving as they babbled and exclaimed, their faces twisted with amazement, excitement, and fear.

Kyte and the guards were still looking around the floor in bewilderment.

"THERE!" Brand howled. "THERE ABOVE YOU, KYTE, YOU DOLT! GUARDS! STOP THEM!"

Rye! Sonia's voice clamored faintly in Rye's whirling mind. *Take us up! Up!*

But Pepper was sobbing, clinging to Rye's back, the hood pinned beneath him. "I'm sorry, Spy!" he was wailing. "I'm sorry. I've killed us all! Oh, Chub . . ."

"Hold on, Pepper!" Rye gasped. "Just hold on! We are out of their reach! Far out of their —"

The words stuck in his throat as there was a violent jerk. He looked down and his jaw dropped in disbelief. A guard had leaped for the trailing end of the rope and had caught it.

But it was impossible! No one could jump so high!

And then Rye remembered. The jump would have been impossible for an ordinary man, certainly. But the Master's guards were not human. Not human! How could he have forgotten?

Up, Rye! Higher! Rye, listen to me!

The guard was clawing at Pepper's feet. But Pepper was protected by the armor shell, and the guard's stubby fingers could not take hold. Rye's skin crawled as another guard leaped, springing straight up from the floor like a huge insect and catching the first guard's ankles. A third gray figure followed him. The fourth did not have to jump. He merely reached up, seized his brother's legs, and tugged till the veins stood out on his low brow.

The guards were heavy. They were enormously strong. They were dragging the rope down. The rope was becoming taut, thinning dangerously as Dirk and Sholto hauled on it with all their might.

The rope will snap, Rye thought dully. Out of the corner of his eye, he saw movement farther along the wall. Kyte's remaining guards were running up the stairs to the empty balcony that hung below the bars.

One by one, the guards hurled themselves at the prisoners dangling from the stretched, motionless rope. One by one, repelled by the armor shell, they bounced back and fell, screaming, to the paving below.

And then Rye saw Kyte almost directly beside him. She had vaulted to the balcony roof. Her quell weapon was in her hand. She grinned and pointed it at him.

"STOP, KYTE!" Brand bellowed. "THEY ARE TOO CLOSE TOGETHER! IF YOU QUELL ONE, YOU WILL QUELL THEM ALL. THE TEST MUST GO AHEAD ON TIME — I SWORE IT TO THE MASTER!"

"The Master will not care if the test is delayed when he hears I have captured *two* enemy spies!" Kyte shrieked. "Spies and *sorcerers*, Brand! Stinking copper-heads! Look at them! And how else am I to catch them but —"

"LOOK HIGHER, YOU FOOL! NEAR THE ROOF! THE TWO PULLING THE ROPE!"

Kyte looked up. Her eyes narrowed, and her lips drew back from her teeth as she recognized Sholto. She thrust the quell back into her belt and snatched another weapon — the stubby black tube she had used to smash the rock at the Diggings.

With a stab of pure terror, Rye saw her swing the weapon up and aim it at his brothers, who were both in clear view, flooded in sunlight and still straining at the rope.

"Dirk! Sholto! Beware!" he shouted.

At the same moment, Kyte fired. But something had gone wrong with her aim. Instead of the charge hitting Dirk and Sholto, it blasted into the wall beside them, shattering the bars and blowing a gaping hole in the smooth gray material below.

Snarling, Kyte fired again. And again. And each time, incredibly, her wrist twisted, so Dirk and Sholto were unhurt, while another great hole was blasted in the wall.

"Let the rope go!" Rye roared. "Dirk, Sholto! Get away!"

The testing hall was echoing with thunderous sound. The giant birds were screeching. Great chunks of the gray wall were crashing onto the paving, and the air was swirling with gray dust. Brand was bellowing at Kyte, his voice rising higher every moment, while beside him the skimmers flapped and fought, clawing at the glimmering walls of their cages.

And still Dirk and Sholto stood, bent to the rope, bathed in sunlight. And still Kyte aimed, fired, and missed, her whole body shaking now, her face a mask of rage and disbelief.

It was a nightmare. A nightmare from which there was no escape.

Rye felt Sonia's hand grip his fiercely. He tore his eyes from his brothers and looked at her.

Sonia's hair was standing out around her head like a mass of copper wires, so bright in the sunlight that it seemed to be shooting sparks. Her face was sharp with exhaustion, her shadowed eyes like deep green pools.

"Witch!" cried Bean, shrinking back from her.

"Save us, Witch!" shouted Bird through chattering teeth.

"I am not the one who can save us," Sonia said huskily, holding Rye's gaze.

Rye, you have the power. Use it!

The voice in Rye's mind pierced the nightmare, sharp as a blade. He felt Sonia's fingers tighten over his hand — the hand that wore the armor shell and the speed ring. The hand that still bore the scar of the sea serpent scale . . .

The hand that clutched the red feather.

Rye thought of the feather, warm against his skin.

He thought of what it meant, what it promised, what he needed. He forgot the skimmers. He forgot the guards, forgot Kyte, forgot Pepper's sobs, and Brand's roars. He forgot his brothers' peril. He thought only of the power he had been given by the Fellan Edelle — the power he alone could use, not just to save himself, but to save them all.

Up! he thought.

And felt himself soaring. Felt dusty air blowing in his face. Saw the roof rushing down to meet him. Heard Kyte's startled yell from below and the explosion of sound as yet another of her charges went wild. Heard the shouts of the guards clinging to the end of the rope as they were jerked upward, their strength and weight nothing to the power of the tiny charm gripped in his hand.

Then he was standing on the narrow ledge where the bars began, blinking in the fierce sunlight pouring through the grating, with Sonia sagging against him and Pepper's arms still locked around his neck. Below him, the guards still swinging on the rope were roaring and snatching uselessly at his heels. Sholto, sweating face filmed with gray dust, white-knuckled hands clinging to the bars for dear life, was at his shoulder, edging gingerly away to give him more room.

And on Rye's other side, separated from him by a swarm of prisoners who had abandoned the rope, was Dirk.

Moment by moment, the swarm was shrinking. Dirk was seizing the prisoners and swinging them high — up toward the hole in the grating, into the enormous hands of Bones. And Bones, his death's head face grinning down through the gap, his impossibly long, thin arms pumping up and down like a tireless machine, was hauling one small, stocky figure after another out onto the roof.

"STOP THEM!" Brand's voice, cracking with panic, echoed through the testing hall. "STOP THEM OR I SWEAR IT IS DEATH TO YOU ALL!"

Dirk was too intent on freeing the prisoners as fast as possible to pay attention. Sholto had his face pressed to the bars, with his back to the room. Sonia, limp with exhaustion, did not raise her head.

So it was only Rye who glanced around, and down, in the direction of Brand's voice. Only he saw the gray-faced supervisor gliding rapidly between two of the huge transparent cages on Brand's balcony, and stretching out her hands to the black circles in the balcony shield.

Rye's throat closed. "Dirk!" he choked. "Sholto! Take hold — take hold of me! Make haste! Oh, make haste!"

The supervisor's wrists turned. Clear round holes opened inside the black-rimmed circles. And in an instant, the cages on either side of her were empty, and the dusty air of the testing hall was alive with shrieking skimmers.

THE ATTACK

Screaming curses at the supervisor, Kyte leaped from the guards' balcony roof and swung into the balcony itself, locking the door behind her. The guards still on the stairway howled and threw themselves at the door, beating on it to no avail. The guards dangling from the end of the rope howled, too — but not for long. They were the first things the skimmers saw. In seconds, they were gone, borne to the ground and overwhelmed by pale, flapping horrors.

"Shut the grating!" Rye heard Sholto bellow.

There was a clang and piteous screams from Chub and the others on the roof as Bones obeyed. Even in that moment of absolute terror Rye's heart swelled with admiration for the brother who could think so clearly and quickly with death staring him in the face.

Of course the opening had to be sealed. Whatever happened in the future, Sholto was determined that his quest would not end with the skimmers escaping the building, killing the people on the roof, then flying on to ravage every living thing in the Scour.

And if Sholto had thought quickly, Dirk had acted just as quickly. With Bird, the only prisoner he had failed to free, tucked under one arm, Dirk had leaped to Rye's side just in time to share the protection of the armor shell.

Half of the skimmers attacked the guards on the stairway. The other half flew at the ledge like furies, spurs dripping venom, needle teeth bared, mud-colored eyes gleaming in the sun. Snapping and snarling, they dashed themselves against armor they could not see, attacking again and again.

The air was thick with them. The hideous flapping of their wings almost drowned out the screeching of the giant birds in the room beyond the bars — the iron bars that weakened the shell's magic. Already, Rye felt bruised. He knew that it would not be long before the buffeting of the skimmers' wings and claws, combined with exhaustion and terror, caused one of his companions to lose hold of him and fall.

Pepper, perhaps — Bird — Sholto . . . even Sonia, if Rye's own strength failed for an instant.

He had to get them away. But if he used the feather to soar with them up through the flap in the grating and onto the roof, the skimmers would follow. It would be impossible to prevent it, once the beasts saw that the grating had a weakness.

266

If only he could distract them. If only there was a way to slow them, to confuse them . . .

He felt Sonia stir weakly against him. Into his mind floated a misty vision of the past — of his mother's beehives, white and square, lining the honey hedge in the garden of the little house in Southwall, and Lisbeth in her beekeeper's veil and gloves bending . . .

And suddenly the air was swirling with smoke — dense, white smoke.

For an instant, Rye could not think where the smoke had come from. Then he realized what must have happened. Somehow Sholto's smoke weapon must have survived the flood. Sholto had remembered it and used it!

The smoke thickened. Rye's eyes began to stream. He heard Dirk, Bird, and Pepper coughing. The skimmers wheeled and slowed, shrieked in confusion, began weaving drunkenly away.

Now!

"Hold on!" Rye shouted, tightening his grip on Sonia.

And as quick as a thought, they were high up in the corner of the hall, pushing through the flap in the grating. And Bones, laughing like a maniac, was dragging them all out into the sun.

All but one.

"No Wanderer," Bones croaked, his grin fading.

Rye's stomach turned over.

267

"Sholto?" Dirk shouted, looking wildly around.

"Not along with you, Wanderer weren't," said Bones miserably. "Bones sees no Wanderer's face in the hole, no Wanderer's hand stretching up for aid. Still down below he be, it seems."

The celebrating people on the roof fell abruptly silent. Chub buried her face in Pepper's shoulder. Bird ran her fingers through her dust-filled hair. Dirk stood up, his face very grim. Only Sonia did not stir. Overcome by exhaustion, she remained huddled where Bones had gently laid her.

They peered down through the grating, into the testing hall. Already the smoke was thinning, but it still filled the whole upper part of the room, masking their view of the floor. The balconies were clouded. The ragged, flapping shapes of the skimmers were just visible below the level of the smoke, like shadows seen through a veil.

"Did he fall?" Chub quavered.

"No!" Dirk exclaimed, dropping to his knees and pointing. "There!"

Sholto was still standing on the ledge, right beside a gaping hole in the wall. He was facing out into the testing hall and looking down. Rye felt a shiver run down his spine as he saw that his brother was smiling.

"Come on, then!" Sholto called, beckoning mockingly. "Here I am! Come and get me!"

Dirk cursed under his breath.

"Ah, Spy's Brother has lost his wits!" moaned Pepper. "He is summoning the beasts!"

But Rye shook his head. He had seen movement on the balcony just below where Sholto was standing. A black shape was crawling up to the balcony roof, standing up.

It was Kyte. Her handsome face was cold with rage. She raised the black tube weapon and pointed it at Sholto.

"NO, KYTE!" Brand's panicking voice echoed from the opposite balcony. "CAPTURE, NOT KILL! DO YOU HEAR?"

Kyte's shoulder twitched, but she did not lower her weapon.

"Your aim has been very poor so far this morning, Kyte," Sholto drawled. "Was the sun in your eyes? Or did it upset you to find your prisoners whisked out from under your nose?"

"He is taunting her deliberately," Dirk muttered. "It is as if he wants her to fire."

"He might think that would be best," said Bird. "The smoke is thinning. The slays will soon be back."

"Don't move, Vrett!" Kyte snarled.

"My name is not Vrett." Sholto's smile broadened. "Have you not worked that out yet? You brought an imposter to the Harbor, Kyte. You carried me here in triumph, boasting of finding me, making it seem that you had tracked me from the shore. Who was going to question me seriously after that? I must thank you, most sincerely, for making my task so easy."

"Well, you've shown your hand now, scum!" spat Kyte. "And for what? For nothing! I'll soon round up the rats you've released, and all their friends, too. I'll make them pay and pay for your treachery!"

"If you survive the Master's anger, which I very much doubt," Sholto said casually, his infuriating smile never wavering. "Rescuing your prisoners was not my main task, you know. The slays on the lower floor are all dead, Kyte — as dead as the real Vrett, whose name badge I used to make a fool of you."

"As dead as you are about to be!" Kyte shrieked, her eyes blazing with rage.

"Ah!" Sholto raised one eyebrow. "Does this mean your kind invitation to breakfast no longer stands?"

Tormented beyond endurance, Kyte bared her teeth and fired. And this time there was no twitching, no sudden jerking of the wrist. This time Kyte fired straight, and instantly fired again, and again, spraying the wall with charges till her weapon was empty and would fire no more.

The wall seemed to explode. The roar was deafening. Shattered bars fell clanging to the floor. Dust billowed up through the grating. As the dust cleared, all the watchers on the roof could see that where Sholto had been standing there was nothing but a vast, dark, crumbling hole.

Bones threw back his head and howled in misery.

Bird's people groaned. Dirk and Rye looked at each other and ran for the flap in the grating.

"No, Spy! Giant, come back!" Bird shouted after them. "He's gone! There's no hope!"

But Rye and Dirk knew there was. They knew their brother. Already Rye was through the grating. Already Dirk was lying with his head and shoulders in the gap, peering after him.

And so it was that they both saw a thin figure edging rapidly along the bars toward them through a haze of smoke and dust. And they both saw what was behind him — what was crawling into the testing hall from the darkness beyond the ruined wall.

The monstrous bird spread its wings. It moved them stiffly at first, then more strongly, beating away the smoke that clouded its view. The spines on the back of its long neck rose. It opened its terrible beak and screeched its fury, its defiance to any order, its ravenous hunger. Then its glassy eye fell on Kyte.

Kyte staggered back, trying to fire, forgetting that her weapon was empty. In terror, she leaped for the stairway. It was her last act. The bird plucked her out of the air, and in an instant, she was gone.

Rye heard Kyte scream but mercifully did not see her horrible death. The moment the giant bird struck, he had launched himself at Sholto, caught him around the waist, and swept him up to where Dirk was waiting.

Only when all three of them were safely together on the roof and the grating was sealed once more did

Rye look down. And what he saw made him understand what had been in Sholto's mind when he taunted Kyte into firing at the damaged wall with such fury that the charges had blasted a hole in the cage behind it.

The giant bird had found new prey. And so had the skimmers — or that was what they seemed to think at first. The battle raging in the air of the testing hall was ferocious. The skimmers were many and used to attacking creatures larger than themselves. But never had they faced a foe like this — a foe with fangs and talons far bigger than their own, wings that crushed bone, and spines like blades.

They were being slaughtered. The sight was ghastly. But what Rye saw when he lifted his eyes to Brand's balcony was worse.

The gray-faced supervisor had gone. The third skimmer cage had been removed. Controller Brand was standing alone, his face pressed to the transparent shield. His body was rigid, lifeless. His eyes were staring, blank and dead. His mouth gaped in a soundless scream. The black box was still gripped in his hands. But now the hands were nothing but sooty, smoking bone.

Shuddering, Rye lifted his head. He discovered Sonia awake and standing beside him, her face expressionless.

"The Master was not happy with the test results, it seems," she said.

Rye looked wordlessly at his brothers.

Dirk swallowed. He was very pale.

"Well, that is the best we can do for now, I think," Sholto murmured, turning away. "Shall we go?"

❋

They left the Harbor in a long, linked line, running like the wind thanks to the magic of the speed ring.

"Hand in hand we goes, like the wizard kings in the old tales!" caroled Bones, his wild white hair blowing back in the breeze. "Ah, this is a day indeed, lords an' lady! This is a day!"

Even he had no breath to say much more. So fast did they make their escape, so anxious were they to put as much distance as possible between themselves and the Harbor, that there was little chance for talk or explanations.

As they sped past the Diggings, some of the questions seething in Rye's mind were answered, at least. The hood of concealment had blown back from his head, but while the Diggings guards sullenly watched from behind the locked gates, they did not come out to block the way or offer a challenge.

" 'Twas the same last evening," panted Bones, looking back over his shoulder. "Bones comes a-running by with Giant feeble as a newborn babe on his arm, an' ol' guards they stand like Saltings stones an' don't stir to stop us! 'Ho!' Bones says to himself. That's what magic ones can do!"

Not magic, Bones, but fear of Kyte, Rye thought, suddenly remembering the slave hunter's last order to the Diggings guards.

"An' there's ol' Four-Eyes, too," Bones went on. "Cheating, lying Four-Eyes, fast sleeping in his steamer wagon outside the gate, an' *he* don't stir neither!"

"The trader?" Sholto said, jolted out of his silence. "He sold me Vrett's coat — Vrett's identity badge was in the pocket, but Four-Eyes had no idea what it was. *And* he gave me a ride to the Diggings, where Kyte found me. I owe a lot to him!"

"He got what he wanted out of you, brother," Dirk said dryly. "Your lantern."

"And a fine painted sign for his wagon," Rye put in.

Sholto raised his eyebrows and nodded.

"Snaffle is still in my pocket," Sonia panted. "She is asleep, I think. She ate all the hoji nuts. What will we do about her?"

"Leave her with us, lady!" Bones laughed. "Ol' Four-Eyes, he'll be back to the Den soon enough, an' won't he be happy when we hand clink over, good as gold?"

He thought for a moment. "Mind you, Cap'll hide other riches well an' truly," he added. "Cap won't trust trader too far, no indeed."

What Bones meant by that was a mystery until, seeing some sign beside the track that no one else could spot, he stopped dead and uncovered his sled. It proved to be heaped with the first goods Chub and Itch had thrown from the trader's wagon.

"Cap, he took ducks afore," Bones chattered as he slid between the sled's shafts. "Cap hears Bones go to find you, lords an' lady. So Cap follows. But all Bones finds is Giant, waking giddy with myrmon, an' food galore a-lying all about. An' Cap comes up an' he says Bones can hide sled an' take Giant on, like Giant says he must. But ducks can't be buried without harm, an' ducks is great treasure from the olden days. So Cap, he carried them back to the Den."

After that, the group ran a little more slowly, with Bones panting along behind. Despite their fears, there had been no pursuit from the Harbor — *not really surprising*, thought Rye, *with Kyte and her guards dead, and Brand dead, too.*

And in time they could run no farther, for a cart drawn by six rangy black goats was coming straight for them, flanked by marching lines of stocky people. The battered sign on the cart's side read:

NANNY'S PRIDE FARM
• Best Milk • Cheese • Honey (in season) •
• Fresh Tarny Roots •

"Bell!" screamed Bird, waving wildly.

"Ho there!" a voice yelled from the cart. "So you saved yourselves, did you? Bless my heart, if I'd known I'd have stayed home and got some sleep!"

As the small people around him cheered and ran to meet the cart, memories of FitzFee again stabbed at Rye. What was FitzFee doing now? How were he and his family faring?

"It is tempting to stay here," Dirk muttered, glancing at Sholto and Rye. "These people would hide us at the farm, I am sure. And now we know that this place is the source of the skimmers. We know the Master is the Enemy of Weld. We could speak to Cap, make plans to raise a rebellion —"

"No! We must go back to Weld first and tell what we have seen," Sholto broke in impatiently. "We destroyed most of the daylight skimmers, and that will delay the Master's plans. Only for a time, but it will give us a breathing space — time to talk to Tallus, to convince the Warden —"

"You are mad if you think you will convince the Warden of anything that will make him uncomfortable," Sonia said flatly.

Sholto stared at her, and then, to Rye's surprise, he slowly nodded.

"Of course you are right," he said quietly. "I —" He hesitated, rubbing his forehead. "I am not usually so stupid, I assure you. But I feel as if I have been in a dream since you and Rye appeared at the Harbor. I still cannot believe what has happened. So many times I thought we were finished. When Kyte fired at us and kept missing, though her aim was famous in the Harbor!"

He shook his head. "And when the supervisor released the skimmers . . . Suddenly there was smoke everywhere! Just what we needed! It took minutes for me to realize that of course Rye's sorcerer's bag would have contained something that made smoke. Smoke is part of a magician's stock in trade!"

Rye turned and gaped at him. "But — but, Sholto, I thought *you* had —"

"And that key that opens any door!" Sholto went on. "The feather that defies gravity! By the Wall, I am not at all sure that I am awake, even now."

"Oh, you are awake," Sonia said cheerfully. She glanced at Rye, willing him to speak. She seemed to have decided that the next move was up to him.

Rye looked into her eyes.

Have faith.

The message came to him like a breath of cool, sweet air.

"I think," he said carefully, "that we should go back to Weld, consult with Tallus, and then —"

He waited till both his brothers were looking at him before going on.

"And then — I think — we should go through the third Door," he said.

"The *wooden* Door?" exclaimed Dirk. "By the Wall, Rye, why? We already know —"

"There are still too many mysteries," Rye said. "Too many things we do not understand. And from the very beginning, the wooden Door has — has beckoned to me. I think . . . I am *sure* . . . it holds the answer."

"I, too," Sonia said, taking his arm.

Rye saw his brothers look at each other. His heart lifted as Dirk nodded, and Sholto shrugged.

"Very well, little brother," Sholto said softly. "We have had our turns. The last one — will be yours."